The Firefighter's Family Secret

Shirley Jump

Recycling programs
for this product may
not exist in your area

978-0-373-65966-1

The Firefighter's Family Secret

Printed in U.S.A.

www.Harlequin.com

New York Times and *USA TODAY* bestselling author **Shirley Jump** spends her days writing romance so she can avoid the towering stack of dirty dishes, eat copious amounts of chocolate and reward herself with trips to the mall. Visit her website at shirleyjump.com for author news and a booklist, and follow her at Facebook.com/shirleyjump.author for giveaways and deep discussions about important things like chocolate and shoes.

Books by Shirley Jump

Harlequin Special Edition

The Barlow Brothers

The Tycoon's Proposal
The Instant Family Man
The Homecoming Queen Gets Her Man

Harlequin Romance

The Christmas Baby Surprise
The Matchmaker's Happy Ending
Mistletoe Kisses with the Billionaire
Return of the Last McKenna
How the Playboy Got Serious
One Day to Find a Husband
Family Christmas in Riverbend
The Princess Test
How to Lasso a Cowboy
Midnight Kiss, New Year Wish
If the Red Slipper Fits...

Visit the Author Profile page
at Harlequin.com for more titles.

To all the unsung heroes in my life, who put out a helping hand to others when they need it most. You make the world a better place.

Chapter One

The last thing Colton Barlow expected while visiting Stone Gap, North Carolina, was for opportunity to come knocking.

He wasn't a man given to living by the seat of his pants, and, in fact, most everyone who knew him would say Colton was deliberate. A planner. A man who set a course and mapped his route carefully. It was how he had always approached a fire on the job—assess the situation, know the risks and variables and plot the battle with care. Rushing into a blaze with no forethought was what got people killed.

And Colton Barlow had already made that mistake.

He'd spent the past six months trying to settle back into his job. Most days he did okay. Some days he was lucky if he could shrug an arm into the heavy turnout coat. But he told himself he was fine, just fine, and everything was on track.

Until the information that upended his life, told him everything he thought he knew about himself was wrong and led him to a small Southern town and three half brothers he hadn't even realized existed until a month ago. For almost thirty years he'd been Colton Williams—his mother's last name—and now it turned out he was a Barlow. That last name still felt like a new pair of shoes—a little uncomfortable, a little odd. Maybe if he kept thinking of himself as Colton Barlow, the name would grow on him.

His family had, so far. He'd finally met the other Barlow brothers—Jack, Mac and Luke—at Jack's wedding last week, and in the process, he stumbled upon a job opening on the Stone Gap Fire Department.

A job he hadn't even been looking for. But once the idea took root in his head of a change, a new start, Colton thought it wouldn't hurt to at least check it out. Maybe at a new department, people wouldn't look at him with eyes filled with a mixture of pity and mistrust. Maybe he could finally leave the shadows behind him and begin again. He'd lost his love for firefighting after the accident, and wondered sometimes if he'd ever get it back. Then he'd talked to Harry and the first glimmers of excitement about his job returned.

That's what had him turning around almost the minute he got home to Atlanta. He'd returned to Stone Gap, both to have a little time to get to know his brothers and father, and to meet with the fire chief for a formal sit-down. Except Fire Chief Harry Washington wasn't a formal sit-down kind of guy, more a walk-and-talk, see-how-it-goes man. Which was why Colton was strolling through downtown Stone Gap, while Harry gave him a guided tour of the town.

"Best apple pie in the county is served right there," Harry said, pointing at a little restaurant on the corner. A bright red-and-white awning above the Good Eatin' Café pronounced the same thing in a dark blue curly script. Harry, a short and slightly pudgy man with a white buzz cut, looked as if he might indulge in the pie on occasion. He had a wide smile, a twinkle in his eyes and a friendly manner, which most everybody in Stone Gap seemed to respond to, given how many people had shouted a hello on their walk so far. "And if you ask Viv real nice, she'll give you an extra scoop of ice cream on top."

So far, Harry had talked about the best place to buy a pair of work boots, how to unclog a drain, the top menu items at Mabel's diner and a whole host of other topics that didn't have a damned thing to do with firefighting. Colton kept expecting some kind of questions about his skill set, but in the half hour since Colton had met Harry at the station and they'd started walking, nothing related to his occupation had come up in conversation. Maybe Harry was a circuitous guy, Colton thought. One who needed to be brought back around to the real reason he was here. "Sir, if you want my résumé—"

Harry put up a hand. "Let me stop you there, son. I don't hire people based on a piece of paper. You and I both know how quickly paper disappears when you set it ablaze. I make my decisions based on the person, not their fancy-dancy credentials."

"But surely you want to know if I have experience—"

Harry squinted in the sun. "Do you like fishing, Colton?"

The non sequitur made Colton stumble over a crack in the sidewalk. He pushed his sunglasses back up his nose and fell back into place beside Harry. "Uh, yes, sir."

Harry nodded. "Good. Go home, grab a pole and meet me down at Ray Prescott's place 'round three this afternoon. We'll do the whole formal interview thing then."

"While we're fishing?"

Harry grinned. "It's called multitasking, son. Now, if you ask my wife, she'll tell you I can't talk and breathe at the same time, and while that may be true, I sure as hell can talk and fish at the same time." He gave Colton a little salute then strode off down the sidewalk toward the brick fire station.

Colton stared after him for a long time, then decided that if he wanted a job in Stone Gap—and he still wasn't sure he did—then he should get a fishing pole. Not that Colton had gone fishing much. A few times with his uncle Tank, but that was about it. He'd been too busy trying to be the man of the family, a job thrust on him from the minute he could walk. Even now, even all these miles away from his mother and sister, he felt that mantle of responsibility. Of course, Katie was all grown up now, and their mother…well, she was what she liked to call "a work in progress."

Which meant Colton shouldn't feel bad about doing something for himself for once. Like going fishing.

Especially considering how much his life had changed in such a short period of time. A month ago he'd been working for the Atlanta FD, spending his free time working on his mother's run-down car and urging his sister to take some time off, live a little, someplace other than the accounting firm where she spent a minimum of eighty hours a week. In return, Katie had needled him about being the quintessential bachelor, with an apartment as empty as a store going out of business. Sure, he had the occasional fling, but he wasn't interested in serious relationships, and he made sure the women he dated knew it. He'd thought his life was more or less complete.

Then he found out that Uncle Tank—his real name was David, but no one ever called the barrel-chested, hearty man by anything other than Tank—whom Colton had always thought was just a family friend, was actually his real uncle, and that his biological father—a man his mother had never spoken about— lived in Stone Gap, along with the three sons he had raised. Robert Barlow had ignored Colton's existence for thirty years, a fact that still stung, even though Colton told himself he was far too old to care whether he'd had a dad to teach him how to complete a layup or tell him how to win a girl's heart.

But he did care. And working through the roller coaster of emotions that meeting his siblings and father had awakened was part of what had kept Colton here in Stone Gap. A saner man might have just turned his back on all of this and left town forever, but Colton had this need to know where he came from. His mother had called it his curiosity gene, the same need that had driven Colton to dismantle the dishwasher when he was eleven, and ask a thousand questions in every class he ever took.

Now he had a thousand and ten questions for Bobby Barlow, but Colton had hesitated to ask them. Had delayed seeing his father again, because Colton wasn't so sure he wanted to hear the answers.

Nor was he so sure his father would want a relationship with him. Colton wasn't the success that Mac was, the war hero Jack was or the second generation partner that Luke was. Sure, Colton was a firefighter, but he was barely hanging on to the job he had in Atlanta after the disaster that claimed two of his coworkers six months ago. A disaster that Colton could have avoided, if only he had tried harder.

The memory of that night had a way of stealing Colton's breath when he least expected it. He'd catch a whiff of smoke or hear a crash, and he'd be there again, screaming into his mask for Willis and Foster. He'd see the burst of flame, hear the crack of the overhead beam, feel the heat crushing his gear. And see the yawning cavern that opened up like a hungry beast and swallowed the best men—and the best friends—Colton had ever known.

He pinched the bridge of his nose and willed the memory back into the shadows. It took a while, four deep breaths to be exact, but then he opened his eyes and reminded himself he was in Stone Gap, North Carolina, on a vacation of sorts. And about to go fishing.

Get it together, Barlow.

He jogged across Main Street, avoiding the lone car going south. He shook his head in amazement. Stone Gap wasn't a hundredth as busy as Atlanta had been. That alone might be a nice change if he got offered a job at the department here.

If he even wanted to stay. Living in Stone Gap, becoming part of the fabric of the community, would mean being around his father on a regular basis. Dealing with all those questions that kept needling at his thoughts, the ones he wasn't ready to face.

At the same time, it would mean having three brothers, three men who were the kind Colton had as friends back home. Three men he already genuinely liked. A lot.

He spied a familiar pair of legs sticking out from under the body of a Ford pickup truck at Gator's Garage, the Barlow family business. Colton hesitated for a moment—this whole thing with his brothers was still so new, he wasn't sure how to handle things like running into Luke downtown—then decided the only thing to do was to just go over there and say hello.

Colton ambled into the garage. He'd always liked garages, the smell of motor oil, the myriad tools, the puzzles of the cars that needed fixing. Gator's used to be run by his father, until Bobby had knee-replacement surgery and needed to slow down. Now Luke was in charge, while Bobby worked part-time.

Colton took in the pegboards filled with tools, the

tall red chests stuffed with parts, and imagined his father here, teaching Luke how to change the oil in a Chevy or rotate the tires on a Ford. The thought made Colton a little envious. Maybe getting to know Luke, Jack and Mac better would help ease some of those feelings. Colton looked down at the work boots below him. "Hey, Luke."

Luke pushed out from under the car and grinned up at Colton. He had the same dark brown wavy hair and blue eyes as the rest of the Barlows, Colton included. Looking at his brothers was eerily like looking in the mirror. "Hey, Colt. Good to see you! Guess we didn't scare you off, after all."

"I'm not so easy to get rid of." He chuckled. "Plus, I had an interview with Harry, the fire chief, so I figured I'd come back here and see it through." Colton shrugged. "Not thinking it's going to lead to anything, but it's a shot. Might as well check it out."

Luke nodded at that, then got to his feet, grabbed a rag and cleaned off his hands. "Glad to hear you're staying a bit. You can help me torture Mac now that Jack is off on his honeymoon. But I have to warn you, Jack and I have a good routine going that keeps Mac at the center of a lot of merciless teasing. You gotta be on your toes to hang with us."

Colton laughed. He liked the relationship the brothers had. Jack, a former soldier, was a good guy, solid and clearly head over heels for his new wife, Meri. Luke was the prankster of the family, though his heart was with his new fiancée, Peyton Reynolds, and their daughter Maddy, while Mac was the overachieving tycoon who had made millions in buying and selling companies, but had recently met and fallen in love with local girl Savannah Hillstrand.

"Sounds like a plan." Colton shook his head. "I still have to get used to having all this family. It's been just me, my sister and my mom for so long, and now all of a sudden, it's like I'm tripping over Barlows."

Luke chuckled. "We're pretty much everywhere. Just ask the neighbors, who blamed every broken window and torn-up lawn on one of us."

"Rightly so?"

"You know it." Luke grinned. "But I'll never admit to the crimes of my youth, at least not in front of my impressionable daughter, who I'm trying to steer away from my mistakes." He made a circle in the air. "So between you and me, I was a Goody Two-shoes."

That made Colton laugh. "And people are going to believe me when I say that?"

"Hell, no. But that's okay. I just blame all my misdeeds on Mac. I love seeing his face get that scrunched-up look." Luke tossed the rag on the counter then grabbed the clipboard that held the day's jobs. "Listen, I'd love to sit around and shoot the breeze, but I have a bunch of work on tap for today. Ever since I took over for Dad, this place has been hopping. What say we grab breakfast tomorrow morning, you, me and Mac?"

"Sounds good." Colton feigned coolness, but he was secretly pretty pleased the other Barlow boys had welcomed him so easily. He didn't expect the road ahead would always be smooth, but he was glad they'd started off so well. His brothers had brought him into the fold as easily as inserting a card into the deck. Maybe if he started with the brotherly relationship, he'd be able to ease into the one with his father. "Hey, where's the best place to get a fishing pole around here?"

Luke grinned. "Let me guess. Did Harry invite you? That man would be a professional fisherman if he could get paid for it. Go on over to Ernie's across the street. They have pretty much everything."

"Thanks." It didn't seem like enough to say to Luke, because it didn't capture all that Colton really wanted to say, but he was a guy, and *thanks* was pretty much the extent of what he was capable of. "See you."

Luke nodded. "See you tomorrow."

Tomorrow. Breakfast with his *brothers*. The word still sounded weird in his head, even weirder when he spoke it aloud. All the things he had lacked all his life, right here in this tiny little town. Yeah, maybe staying a while was a good idea.

He ducked into Ernie's Hardware & Sundries, which sported a hand-drawn sign advertising a special on night crawlers. Colton waited a second for his eyes to adjust to the dim interior, the rows of shelves and the bins of garden tools.

"Good morning. Can I help you?"

He turned toward the lilting sound of a woman's voice. That was what hit Colton first—her voice, which, even in those few syllables, seemed to have a sweet, happy tone to it, as if his coming into the store was the best thing that had happened to her all day.

Then he saw her, and decided maybe seeing her was

the best thing that happened to *him* all day—because the woman behind the counter was stunning.

His grandmother would have called her *willowy*. She was tall and thin, with long, straight, light blond hair that was so pale it seemed ethereal. Her dark green eyes were wide and deep, and matched by a welcoming smile that made him feel warm inside. She wore a white button-down shirt with big silver buttons with the sleeves rolled up, tucked into a pair of dark jeans that hugged her curves.

"Uh…yeah, good morning," Colton said, wondering when he'd become a guy who stammered. "I'm looking for fishing rods?"

"Right this way." She crooked her finger, beckoning to him, and made her way down one of the aisles. He would have followed her to Timbuktu with just that one gesture. Not to mention the view he had from behind.

She stopped in the middle of the aisle and waved toward a display of tackle and fishing poles. "I don't know what you're looking for, but if you were to ask my dad, he'll tell you the best one is this graphite bait caster right here. Lot of folks go for this spinning combo—" she pointed to another, fancier pole "—but my dad always says that the right pole sits in your hand like it was made for your palm. Not too heavy, not too light, and when you go to pull up on the hook, the pole does the work."

It was all pretty much Greek to him. "Okay, let me see one of the graphic things."

"Graphite." She grinned at his mistake then handed him the pole. "It also matters where you're fishing and what you're fishing for."

"Well, I don't really know the second answer. I'm meeting Harry Washington over at Ray Prescott's place. It's a job interview. Sort of."

She laughed. "I know Harry. He's not much on formalities. Ray's place is right on the water, so chances are you're doing a little surf fishing. That's a different animal from fishing in the lake. You might want to try this pole instead." She pulled yet another from the seemingly endless rack. "It's got a heavier reel. That will help you if you're going for some striped bass or red drum. And the gear is heavy enough, in case you accidentally hook a shark."

He took the new pole she handed him and hefted it in his palm. It seemed strong, solid. "Sounds like you know what you're talking about."

She turned and gave him a grin. "Well, when you're daddy's girl, and the only kid at that, you play soccer and catch fish and learn how to shoot a rifle. At the same time you're learning how to curl your eyelashes and pick out lipstick and wear high heels."

He chuckled then put out his hand. "I think with a line like that, we should be formally introduced. I'm Colton. Colton...Barlow." The name sounded strange still, but it was beginning to grow on him.

Confusion muddied her eyes. "One of *the* Barlows? With Jack, Luke and Mac?"

Small-town living, Colton thought and grinned. "Sort of. I'm their half brother. From Atlanta. Firefighter, novice fisherman and decent first baseman."

He didn't know what made him give her that mini-résumé, but then she laughed, and it made his day.

"Pleased to meet you, Colton Barlow from Atlanta. I'm Rachel Morris, daughter of the famous Ernie. Expert fisherwoman and not-bad shortstop."

"Maybe you could teach me a thing or two about catching the right one."

Her smile reached into her eyes, lighting up her entire face. A flirty, teasing look in those green depths toyed with the edges of her lips. "Is that what you're here for? Because we don't sell matches made in heaven. Just fishing poles and garden rakes."

"I'm just talking trout and bass." He picked up another pole from the ones she'd pointed out to him, hefted it for weight, put it back and reselected the one she'd given him. From feel at least, it seemed like Rachel's choice was the best. "Definitely not long-term commitments."

"Just what this town needs. Another confirmed bachelor." But she laughed when she said it, took the fishing pole from him and walked back to the register. She punched in a few keys then recited the price and thanked him when he handed over a credit card.

While she was finishing the transaction, Colton racked his brain for something else to say. Something to prolong the moment before he had to leave. He liked Rachel. Found her intriguing. And it had been a long, long time since he'd met a woman who interested him like that. "So, have you lived here all your life?"

Yeah, way to go on the lame question. Clearly, he was out of practice.

"Pretty much. I was born and bred here." She printed out the credit card receipt and handed the white slip of paper to him, along with a pen. "Are you thinking about moving here? If you get the job with the fire department?"

"Maybe."

"Still testing us out, huh?" She grinned. "Well, I can tell you this much about Stone Gap. It defines small town. If you sneeze over your Wheaties at breakfast, half the town is lined up for a flu shot by lunchtime. Most everyone here grew up in each other's pockets, as my dad likes to say. Which means everyone knows pretty much everything about everyone else."

"Sounds…suffocating."

"It can be." She shrugged. "But in a small town, someone's always there if you need help. If you're down, there's a neighbor or a friend to pull you back up. Stone Gap has its faults, like any place, but at its core, it's a great town to live in. And you can't beat the weather or the fact that we're right on the water."

He chuckled. "Are you with the welcoming committee?"

She blushed, a soft pink that stole across her cheeks. "No, I just…finally learned to appreciate this place."

"I've never lived in a place that I loved like that. Atlanta's fine, but it's a big city. You can get…lost there pretty easily." His voice trailed off, and he shook his head.

"Lost in more ways than one?" she said softly.

Colton cleared his throat. He wasn't about to unload his life history in a hardware store with a woman he barely knew. Even if every time she smiled, she made him want to linger for hours on end. "Well, thanks for the tips about Stone Gap. I'll keep them in mind."

"Sure. Anytime. And if you want the twenty-five-cent tour, you know where I am."

"Twenty-five cents? That's it?"

She blushed again. "It's a small town."

That made him laugh. "Harry already told me where the best apple pie is."

"Then you're down to the twenty-cent tour. Unless you have already discovered the best place for making out." The blush intensified. "I meant, for the teenagers."

"Of course." Making out? That made him think about climbing in the backseat of his car with Rachel and seeing where it might lead. Not a good train of thought to follow, but that didn't stop him from a quick mental image. "Us old people are too mature for that."

"Definitely."

Yet everything in the undercurrent of their conversation said differently. He might be out of practice in the dating arena, but he sensed some definite attraction in the air. He had the strangest urge to lean across the counter and kiss her right now.

"Uh, I should sign this." He bent his head and scrawled his name across the receipt then handed it back to her.

"Thanks," she said. She lifted the fishing pole and gave it to him. "Need anything else?"

Your phone number, his brain whispered. Because he definitely wanted to get to know Rachel Morris, fisherwoman and shortstop, much better. But he was leaving in a few days, so asking her out wouldn't make any sense.

But as he headed out of the store, Colton had to wonder if maybe forgoing her number was the thing that didn't make any sense, because she lingered in his mind long after he cast the first line into the water.

Chapter Two

Rachel dusted shelves that didn't need dusting and tidied displays that were already tidy. It was a Tuesday, one of the least busy days in her dad's shop. Her only customer had been the tall, good-looking firefighter in a faded blue T-shirt and stonewashed jeans that hugged his legs and told her Colton Barlow was a man who worked out. A lot. Good Lord, his biceps alone were enough to make her mind start fantasizing. Hot and yummy, and a definite change from the older, potbellied retirees who usually came into the store.

Men who looked like Colton Barlow, and had a killer smile like his, didn't come to Stone Gap very often. He'd stayed long enough that she almost thought he was going to ask her out. But in the end, he just paid for his purchase and headed out the door. Clearly, she'd read him wrong. Of course, she hadn't helped things by being such a dork and blushing every five seconds, or making that stupid comment about the best place to make out. It was as if she was back in high school again and crushing on the cute boy in English class.

She shouldn't have been disappointed—after all, she was the one who had sworn off men until she had more than five minutes of free time a day—but she was. It would have been nice, really nice, if he'd noticed more than just the type of rod and reel she was selling him.

At six she locked up, got in her car and drove across town to the three-bedroom bungalow where she'd grown up. The flower beds were overrun with weeds, the trees in desperate need of trimming and the white picket fence out front had faded to a dingy gray. It was as if time had stopped in that house, and now everything else was slowly giving up the fight.

Rachel sighed, parked her car in the drive then headed inside. Just like the outside, the interior of the house was dark and dingy, coated with a fine layer of dust and despair.

Before her mother's death, her father had been at his store day in and day out, clocking in when the shop first opened and staying as long as anyone needed to buy something from him. Her mother had manned the ship at the house, keeping up with the plants and dishes and creating a home with everything she did.

But then cirrhosis had taken Rachel's mother last year, leaving all of them with a hole too wide to fill. It had hit Ernie especially hard. He'd made himself a hermit in the house, losing interest in the store, in fishing, in his life. For that entire year, Rachel had run the shop single-handedly, putting her own life on hold, leaving her father to grieve while she ordered supplies and paid bills and swept the floors.

For ten months he hadn't asked her a single question about how the store was doing. But she'd come by every day nonetheless and given him a recap. Then one day he'd called her in the middle of the day, asked her how it was going. It wasn't much, but her father's spark of interest had given Rachel hope that maybe, just maybe, she could get back to her own venture someday soon. Assuming she still had one, given the dent one year of not working had made in her bridal business. Just when Happily Ever After Weddings was getting off the ground, Rachel had to put it all to the side. She'd lost several bookings, and had probably given up all the ground she had worked so hard to gain the year before. But her father had needed her, and that was all that mattered.

Someday he'd be back in charge, and she'd go back to her life. Someday.

She found her father sitting at the kitchen table, a crossword puzzle in front of him. He had filled in only a handful of clues since she'd left him this morning in the same place, with the same folded section of newspaper in his hands. The breakfast dishes still sat in the sink, and there was nothing in the stove for dinner. Rachel worried that if she ever stopped coming by, her father would stop eating altogether. It was as if losing his wife had made him lose his motivation to move forward. Move anywhere, period.

"Good evening, Dad." She pressed a kiss to his unshaven cheek. She missed the scent of his cologne, the smoothness of his skin after he shaved. "What's for dinner?"

"I...uh...haven't thought about it." He blinked, his eyes bleary and red, probably from getting a few fitful hours of sleep in the recliner in front of the TV. His white hair stuck up on his head, and his T-shirt looked as though it hadn't been washed in a month. "The day goes by so fast sometimes. I didn't even realize it was that time already."

"Why don't I just throw some chicken on the grill?" Rachel pulled open the fridge and pulled out a package of meat, acting like everything was okay. That it didn't make her heart hurt to see her once robust and busy father sitting here like a lump of clay. "You still have those potatoes?"

"Potatoes?"

"I bought them at the store yesterday. Remember?"

"Oh, yeah. I forgot about them. Well, I haven't eaten any potatoes, so they're probably in the bin in the pantry. You know, where Mom always kept them? Never store them with the onions, she'd said, but I can't remember why." He shook his head then turned back to the crossword. "What's a five-letter word for *in fashion*?"

"Umm..." She thought about it while she sprinkled some seasoning on the chicken, then dug in the bin in the pantry, unearthed a few potatoes, washed them and pricked their skins. "Try *vogue*."

"Works for me." He penciled it in. "Been working on this crossword all day. It's a tough one."

It was what he said every day. She wasn't quite sure how her father spent the hours between breakfast—when she got here at eight and put his coffee on and fixed him some eggs—and six fifteen, when she got back from the store. She didn't want to think of him sitting at this kitchen table, staring out the window, mourning. But truth be told, that was what she knew her father probably did every day.

"Have you called Daryl? He was in the other day. Said he wanted to get you up to the lake, see what's biting." Her father's best friend had been in almost every day over the last month, checking to see if Ernie might have come in for the day. Daryl had tried calling and coming by the house, but if Ernie didn't want to deal with someone, he just ignored them. Rachel hoped that if she kept on mentioning Daryl and her father's favorite pastime, it might get him out the door.

Her father waved that off. Again. "Maybe when the weather is better."

Rachel glanced out the window at clear skies, a sunlit day. "Today was a great day for fishing, Dad."

That made her think of the firefighter again. Colton Barlow. Novice fisherman. Decent first baseman. And very hot guy in general. She wondered how his fishing trip had gone, and whether he'd be back to the store. Whether he'd ask her for coffee—

Then she glanced at her father and realized she probably didn't have time to date. Heck, she barely had time to take care of herself. There were dishes to do, laundry to process, some weeding to tackle, then she had to go home and take care of her own chores, sleep, get up, work the store and come back to her father's house again. Rinse and repeat, day after day, until her father got back into his life. "Dad, I'm going to get this on the grill, then I'll come back in and do the dishes."

"You don't have to. They can keep." He never even looked up from the crossword. "I'll do them later."

She sighed. It was what he always said, whenever she offered to clean for him, but he never swept or washed or did anything about the mess inside the house or the weeds out front. And all the other thousand little things that had gone undone for months.

She put the chicken on the grill then came back inside. She fished out the register report from her pocket and smoothed the paper on the table in front of her father. "Here's today's tally. Things were a little slow." She didn't mention that her only customer had been the firefighter.

The store had barely been surviving in the last few months, but she never told her father that. If she did, his disappointment—in the store, in her—would likely make him retreat even further. So she tried to keep things upbeat, positive. There were days when even that was a challenge.

Her father gave the paper a glance. "Business will pick up."

He'd been saying that for months. But business had dropped to a dangerous low, and right now it was costing more to keep the lights on than she was taking in during the day. She was doing her best, but the people of Stone Gap loved her dad, came to him for his expertise, the way he made everyone feel welcome. She was trying, but she wasn't Ernie. "I think everyone misses you down at the shop."

"I'll be by." His focus was back on the crossword. "Someday."

Rachel slipped into the seat opposite her father and put a hand over her dad's. "Someday...like tomorrow? Come on, Dad. It'll be good for you to—"

He shoved the chair back so fast, it squealed against the tile floor. "I'm fine right here. So let it go."

Then he stomped out of the room, down the hall and into his bedroom. The door shut with a slam, and Rachel was left alone, with the same mess she'd been trying to clean up for the past year.

She fixed the chicken, did the dishes and processed a load of laundry. Then she left her dad a covered plate and a note that said she loved him before she headed out the door. Rachel sat in her car for a long time, debating whether to go home and do the same at her house, then work on the books and orders for the store.

Or maybe, for once, do something for herself.

That made her think of Colton again. He was here on vacation, she presumed. Did that mean he was out tonight? Sitting on a bar stool somewhere, or still fishing? Or was he the type to fill his evenings with a long run or a good novel?

When was the last time she had done any of the above? Had enough time to buy a book, never mind read one? Take a long, lazy walk on a warm summer evening? Sleep in on a Sunday and dawdle over the paper with a cup of coffee and a cinnamon roll?

As she neared the street toward the cozy apartment she lived in, she saw the sign for the Sea Shanty. She debated at the stop sign then finally turned left, away from home and toward the restaurant. She rolled down the windows, let in the ocean breeze and tasted the short burst of freedom in the air.

The Sea Shanty wasn't much, as restaurants went, but the food was good, and they'd recently started featuring live bands almost every night of the week. Rachel picked up her phone, pressed a button and waited for the other end to answer. "You up for a glass of wine and way too many calories?"

"Hell, yes." Melissa, Rachel's best friend since grade school, let out a throaty laugh. "Tell me where and when, and I'll get Jason to watch these kids so I can escape the shackles of motherhood for a few minutes."

"The Sea Shanty. As soon as possible."

"Hold on a sec." Melissa covered the phone then yelled to Jason, "I'm going out so you've got the rugrats for dinner." Then she was back. "Give me ten minutes."

"I can't wait." Rachel pulled into the lot, parked her car and tucked her keys in her purse. How long had it been since she'd had dinner and drinks with friends? Clearly, way too long if she couldn't remember. She had to find a better way to balance her life. Otherwise, she had a feeling she'd wake up a year from now and realize she was still in the exact same place as before. She wanted to date again, go out more often, get her business running. Coming here tonight instead of going home was a good first step, but Rachel had a feeling she was going to need a miracle if she wanted to carve more than an impromptu dinner out of an already tightly structured twenty-four hours.

Yeah, definitely a miracle. She still had a pile of paperwork to do at home, the end of the quarter financials to finalize and a restock order to process. She didn't have time for a long dinner—maybe a quick bite and the rest to go. Melissa would understand, Rachel hoped. Maybe in a few more months…

But even Rachel didn't hold out hope for that. Her father was all she had left, and there was no way she was going to abandon him. If it took one year or ten, she would be there, taking care of him and doing what she should have done—

Before her mother died.

The guilt rolled through Rachel like a wave. Those two years after her mother got sick, Rachel had been so invested—too invested—in her own life. Her father hadn't even told her about her mother's illness early on, and she'd missed all the subtle clues that something was awry. Rachel had been pouring herself into her new business, into getting it off the ground, and by the time she realized her mother was sick—

It was too late.

Her father had been the one who had dealt with the doctor's appointments, the long, sleepless nights, the funeral plans at the end. Her mother had told her, just before the end, that she had begged Ernie not to tell Rachel about the cirrhosis, because she wanted her daughter to be happy, unburdened by an illness that took full-time caregiving. Her father had agreed, and the two of them had done their best to shield their daughter from the situation until the weakness and changes in her mother's face spoke the truth.

That was why Rachel had dropped everything to be there for her father now. She may have let him down before, but she wasn't going to do it again, regardless of how long it took.

The Sea Shanty was half filled with diners, and several people sat at the outdoor bar. Rachel opted for an outdoor table, since the weather was warm, the breeze light, the ocean waves lapping at the shore like a quiet song in the background. The band was tuning up, a three-piece group she'd heard before and liked. They did a lot of covers of popular songs, but had a strong female singer who could belt out a ballad, too.

Rachel was just opening her menu when she caught a glimpse of Colton Barlow, just settling down at the end of the bar. He ordered a beer then picked up a menu.

Damn, he was a good-looking man. He'd changed since this morning, into a fresh pair of jeans and a pale blue polo shirt that stretched across the muscles in his back. His dark hair was damp, which had her picturing him in the shower. Naked. Soapy.

Crap, crap. He'd turned and caught her looking. She jerked the menu up to her face and prayed Melissa arrived, like right now. Instead, Colton slipped off the bar stool, crossed the wooden deck toward her and, in less time than it took to flip a burger, derailed all of Rachel's careful plans.

The pretty clerk from the hardware store blushed when Colton approached. He liked that. She'd come across as so self-assured in the shop, and yet when he caught her eye now, a shy smile flitted across her face, and she dropped her attention to her menu. Avoiding him? Or embarrassed that he had caught her staring?

"You seem to be everywhere I am," he said. Not exactly a winner as far as opening lines went, but in his defense, he was a little rusty. It had been at least three months since he'd been on a date, almost a year since he'd been in anything remotely approaching a relationship.

"It's a small town. It's bound to happen." She put her menu to the side and crossed her hands on the table. All business now, the last traces of her blush gone. "So how was the fishing?"

"Great. The rod you sold me worked out well. Caught two striped bass, but no sharks."

"Just as well," she said, and a smile flitted across her face. "If you got bit while you were staying here, it might put a dent in our tourism industry."

He arched a brow. "Stone Gap has a tourism industry?"

"Well, only if you count the Fullertons, who come down every winter to vacation with the Whitmans." Then she glanced at him again, and her cheeks grew pink. "Well, them…and you, of course."

"Of course." He looked down and noticed another place setting and a second menu at the seat across from her. For a date? Colton had no right to care whether Rachel was dating anyone or not, but a part of him did. He knew he should just let the conversation drop, let her go. He was leaving town in a few days, after all, and anything he started with this beautiful woman he would never be able to finish. Except he couldn't seem to get his feet to move. "I wanted to thank you for the fishing advice you gave me."

She waved that off and gave him a smile. A genuine one that brightened her eyes, her whole face. Something deep inside Colton warmed. "It was nothing. The advice comes free with the purchase of the rod and reel."

Maybe so, and maybe she wasn't interested in him, but in that moment Colton decided he wasn't going to walk away with regret a second time. So maybe he was only going to be in town for a short while. And maybe she was waiting on a man. But he loved the way she smiled and especially loved the way she blushed, and he didn't want to return to his seat without knowing when he was going to see her again. "Let me take you to lunch tomorrow."

"Oh, I can't." She shook her head. "I'm working and it's…difficult for me to get away."

"Then dinner."

"I have… I, uh, don't think I can. I'm sorry." Another head shake, this one a little slower and sadder.

"Are you just playing hard to get?" He grinned. "Or are you really this busy?"

"No, really, I am this busy. My life is…complicated right now."

"Join the club. Mine is a bit of a mess." He glanced again at the second place setting and decided maybe she simply wasn't interested in him. "I'm sorry. I should let you get back to your date."

"Good Lord, don't do that. This poor girl hasn't had sex in months."

Rachel turned red as a beet. Colton spun around to find a short brunette with a big smile and an even bigger purse pulling out the second chair. She thrust a hand toward him. "I'm Melissa, her married best friend. Who is desperately trying to get Rachel back into the dating scene again before she shrivels up and dies like a prune. And you are…single and employed?"

He laughed. "Yes to the first, and sort of to the second. Colton Barlow. I'm a firefighter in Atlanta."

Melissa grinned up at Colton, then shot another grin at Rachel. "He's cute, did you notice?"

Rachel looked as though she wanted to run from the restaurant. So Colton pulled up another chair, spun it backward and straddled the seat. Which only made Rachel blush harder and piqued Colton's interest more. "Maybe," he said. "Seems like a nice enough town. With a lot of nice people."

Melissa nodded. "Very nice. Rachel here is—"

"Trying to order dinner," Rachel cut in. "Did you look at the menu yet, Melissa?"

Melissa waved a hand in dismissal. "I know the menu here. It never changes. Whereas the population of Stone Gap, well, looks like that is changing. And weren't you just saying the other day that there were no good men to date in this town?"

Rachel choked on her water. Colton choked back a laugh then cleared his throat.

"Then maybe you should take me up on my lunch invitation," Colton said to Rachel. "So you can eliminate one more single man from the list."

"He asked you to lunch?" Melissa said. She leaned across the table. "And you said no? Why on earth did you say no?"

"I'm busy and—" Rachel threw up her hands. "I am not having this discussion. I'm ordering some food." She signaled to the waitress. A young blonde came bouncing over to the table, readying a pad of paper.

"What can I get you?" the girl said. She chewed a stick of gum while she talked, which added a snap to each syllable.

"I'd like the fish tacos," Rachel said. "And a glass of chardonnay. Melissa?"

But Melissa wasn't paying attention. She was staring at Colton as if he was the last man on earth and she was going to wrap him up and deliver him to Rachel for Christmas. "Did you say Barlow? As in related to Mac, Jack and Luke?"

He nodded. "They're my half brothers."

"Well, then, that's a whole other vote in your favor. Everybody loves the Barlows." Melissa leaned in toward Colton and lowered her voice. "Rachel is a bit… stubborn, and she is busier than anyone I've ever met, but believe me, she is worth whatever hell she puts you through to date her."

"Melissa!"

"What? I'm just making a case for you." Melissa grinned. She turned to the waitress, who was standing there, tapping her pen on her pad. "Bring me the seafood salad. Those darn kids have left me on a perpetual diet. And for the gentleman—"

"Who isn't staying," Rachel cut in.

"See what I said? Stubborn." Melissa grinned at Colton. "But don't let that... Oh, look. It's Bobby and Della."

Colton turned and saw his father, standing by the hostess station with another couple, and Della, his wife—and the mother of the other Barlow boys. At the same time, Bobby noticed Colton, and he stiffened. He whispered something to Della, and she turned toward Colton. She worked up a smile and gave Colton a little wave.

Colton stared toward Bobby, but a pained look filled his father's face. The other couple, unaware of the tension filling the restaurant, started chatting with Bobby. He gave Colton a half nod then turned his attention back to the people he was with. A second later the hostess gathered up a pile of menus and started waving toward a table on the far end of the room.

A deep ache started in Colton's chest. The father he'd always wanted, the father he had finally found, and despite the auspicious beginning they'd had at Jack's wedding, Colton could tell Bobby still looked uncomfortable with the idea of welcoming his illegitimate son into the family fold.

It was a small town, after all, and that meant they would inevitably run into each other. Colton told himself he hadn't expected a warm, familial welcome, but—

He had. He'd hoped for some Hollywood reunion, with his father trotting him around town with pride, telling everyone that Colton was his son.

A son who let two of his best friends die in a fire? Did you really think he'd want to spread that *news?*

Colton shook off the thoughts. If he let the guilt in, he knew it would take over every thought, and he'd be stuck in that limbo he'd barely climbed out of. He needed to move forward, make a new start. Not dwell on the past and choices he couldn't undo.

"I'll let you ladies enjoy your dinner," Colton said, then got to his feet. He crossed over to Bobby and Della as they made their way through the room, thinking maybe he had misread the look on Bobby's face. But no, the closer Colton drew, the more Bobby's face pinched, and the deeper the dread sank in Colton's gut.

"Hi, Colton," Della said. She was a warm and welcoming woman with dark copper hair and a wide smile. Colton had liked her on the spot. If there was one word he associated with Della Barlow, it was grace. Despite finding out her husband had had an affair, and that the relationship had produced a child, Della had treated him as one of the family. For that, Colton was grateful.

"Yeah, uh, hi," Bobby said. The five of them had

stopped in the center of the restaurant, twenty feet from the empty table. "Nice to see you again, Colton."

A tall, thin man with glasses as round as salad bowls looked over at Colton with a mixture of familiarity and confusion. "Come on and join us, son." The man squinted. "Wait. Are you Mac?"

"No. I'm Colton."

"Colton?" The man looked at Bobby. "Who's Colton? One of the cousins?"

"Yeah, uh, look, why don't you go grab the table, Jerry? Della and I will be right there."

"Sure, sure." Jerry and his wife took a seat at the table and accepted menus from the hostess. They sent over one more confused glance in Bobby's direction.

"How...how are you?" Bobby said.

"Good. Pretty much the same as yesterday."

"That's good." Bobby shifted his weight. "Uh, you're staying in town?"

"For a few days, yeah."

He waited for his father to invite him over, to ask him to join them for dinner. Instead, Bobby glanced over at his friends then back at his son. "Uh, Colton, we need to..." Bobby waved toward the table across the room with that pinched look in his face again.

One of the cousins, that's what his father had agreed Colton was. If anything told Colton where he ranked in his father's life, that did it. Why was he still here? Why was he still hoping for a miracle that wasn't going to come?

"Well, good to see you. Enjoy your dinner." Colton turned away then fished a twenty-dollar bill out of his pocket, tossed it on the bar and walked out of the Sea Shanty. He'd been a fool for coming to this town and thinking he could manufacture a father-son relationship out of thin air. And an even bigger fool for thinking if he stayed any longer he might find all the things he'd been looking for.

Rachel watched Colton exit the restaurant and told herself she was relieved. She didn't have time, after all, for a relationship. And especially not one with a man who wasn't going to be here for more than a few days.

"That was one delicious hunk of man," Melissa said. "Tell me again how you met him?"

"He came into my father's store. Bought a fishing pole." She shrugged.

"Well, I think that's an auspicious start already."

Rachel laughed. "Auspicious start? I wasn't aware anything was started."

"Then you didn't see the look the two of you exchanged." Melissa arched a brow. "Definitely something started. And he's interested in fishing—"

"He bought one pole. A couple of things for tackle. Said he hadn't fished in a long time."

"Close enough to interested." Melissa leaned forward. "Did you give him all the ins and outs of pole handling?"

Rachel laughed. "Did you really just say that? 'The ins and outs of *pole handling*'?"

Melissa grinned. "What? I'm stuck at home with kids all day. When I do get out, it's like I got a free pass from the warden. I get in all kinds of trouble."

Rachel laughed. "Is that what we're doing tonight? Getting into all kinds of trouble?"

"Well, my trouble can only last till nine o'clock. Then this pumpkin has to haul her butt home because the baby will be up at the crack of too early." Melissa let out a long sigh. "Anyway, enough about my pre-ball Cinderella life. How are you doing?"

"I'm good."

Melissa arched a brow. "This is me you're talking to, remember? You've had a lot on your shoulders lately, and I worry about you putting everyone else first and yourself at the bottom of a very long list."

"Spoken like an expert." Rachel grinned.

"True." Melissa laughed. Her friend was always running her kids here there and everywhere, rarely finding enough time to go shopping or get her hair done. "I'm just as bad. The way I see it, all us kettles and pots need to stick together, since we're all in the same boat."

That made Rachel burst out laughing. "That is the worst mash-up of trite phrases I've ever heard."

"Hey, everyone has to have a special skill." Their food arrived, and while they ate, they exchanged small talk about Melissa's kids, several friends they had in common and the hardware store.

A little while later, Melissa glanced at her watch and let out a sigh. "Sadly, it's time for this pumpkin to hit the road. Maybe we can grab coffee later in the week? Two of the kids are in a summer camp, which means

I actually have freedom. Or at least as much freedom as a mom with a baby strapped to her hip can get."

"You love those kids and you know it."

A sweet smile stole across Melissa's face. It was the smile of someone in a secret club, one where only those who had children knew the password and the handshake. For a second envy rolled through Rachel. How she wanted the same for herself, for her own life. Considering she wasn't even dating, never mind married, that kind of thing was going to have to wait. Besides, she had enough on her plate, as Melissa had said, with her father and trying to run his business, while also stealing a minute here and there to keep her own afloat.

They paid the bill and walked outside together. The fireman was nowhere to be seen, and Rachel told herself she wasn't disappointed. But she was.

Melissa gave her a tight hug. "Promise me you'll take time for yourself this week," she said.

"I don't have—"

"You do," Melissa said. "If I have five minutes for a little girl time and an extra-long shower, then you can find a couple hours to go out to dinner with a hot fireman."

"How do you know I want to go out to dinner with Colton?"

"I may be a tired, worn-out mommy and a wife who hasn't had a conversation with my husband in months that hasn't been interrupted by someone puking or yelling, but even I can still recognize interest when I see it." Melissa gave her a hug. "Life is a train, Rachel. You gotta reach out and grab on for the ride before you miss it entirely."

Chapter Three

Scrambled eggs.

Who would have thought all three of the Barlow boys sitting in a booth at the Good Eatin' Café would have the exact same taste in breakfast? Two eggs, scrambled, wheat toast, bacon, extra crispy. Luke, Mac and Colton had recited their orders then laughed when they parroted each other. Even Viv, the owner of the diner, couldn't resist a chuckle. "Do you boys know that is the exact same breakfast your father orders when he's here on Sunday mornin'? Y'all are a bunch of peas in a pod."

Luke chuckled as Viv walked away. "Guess we have a lot in common," he said to Colton. "Let me guess. Your favorite pizza is—" he put a finger to his lips and feigned thought "—pepperoni."

Mac gave Luke a gentle slug. "Everyone loves pep-peroni."

"Well, everyone in *our* family does." Luke arched a brow in Colton's direction. Outside, rain began to fall in a curtain. In seconds the sunny day turned gray, and the pavement was speckled with fast-forming puddles. "Am I right?"

Colton grinned. "Yup. Though the real question, and the one that determines if we're brothers is…" He glanced at Luke and Mac. "Red Sox or Yankees?"

"Oooh, them's fightin' words," Luke said. "Every-body with a brain knows the Yankees are the only team worth cheering for."

Mac scoffed. "And that's why I'm the smart one. The Red Sox are the best ball team. Hands down."

Luke and Mac turned to Colton. "Fess up. Which one do you root for?"

Colton started to answer when the door to the diner opened and Rachel walked in. She was wearing a pale yellow sundress and her hair was tied back in a po-nytail. She shook off the rain, brushing the drops off her bare arms. Even damp from getting caught in the storm, she looked…fun. Like something he'd been looking for and didn't know he wanted to find until he saw it. "I'll be back in a second."

He heard his brothers' laughter as he left the table and went over to Rachel. She was just slipping onto one of the counter stools when he reached her and dropped into the empty seat beside her. "Good morning."

She turned to him with a slight lilt of surprise in her brows and a smile toying with the edge of her lips. "Good morning. You seem to be everywhere I go lately."

He put up his hands. "I swear, I'm not stalking you."

She laughed. He liked her laugh. It was light, airy, sweet. "It's okay. Sometimes living here feels like living in a circle. I run into the same people, at the same time, in the same places."

"That's the complete opposite of Atlanta. Outside of work, I rarely run into people I know. It's kind of like being invisible."

"And do you like that?"

"I don't know. I haven't lived anywhere else before. So I guess I don't know what I really want or like in a place to live. I do know that it's nice to be in a place where life is a little slower. I feel like I can…" He shook his head. "God, I'm going to sound all sentimental if I say this."

"Say what?"

She seemed so interested that he figured even if he did sound like a total dork, it would be okay. "Here, I feel like I can stop and smell the roses." He chuckled. "Seriously, I'm not normally this sappy. Must be the rain."

"Or maybe Stone Gap is rubbing off on you. Before you know it, you'll be taking the chief's job offer and buying a house."

"How do you know Harry offered me a job?"

"It's a small town, Colton, remember?" She grinned. He liked her smile. Liked it a lot. A part of him ached to reach out and trace the sweet curve of her lips.

"Word spreads, especially when there's a hot eligible firefighter in town."

He grinned. "You think I'm hot and eligible?"

A faint blush filled her cheeks. "Well, people think you are. That's what I hear."

He wanted to know if she was one of those people. If she wanted to kiss him even half as bad as he wanted to kiss her. He wanted to see her again, wanted to spend a long, lazy afternoon with her. He fished in his pocket and pulled out a coin. "Here," he said, taking her hand and dropping it into her palm.

She gave him a grin. "What's this for?"

"Prepayment for the twenty-five-cent tour of Stone Gap."

Rachel laughed and started to hand back the coin. "That was just a joke. And I really am swamped right now. I don't think I even have time for the nickel tour."

He closed his hand over hers. "Keep it. And if a hole opens up in your schedule, I'd love to see Stone Gap from your perspective."

Electricity arced in the space between them. It was only a quarter, and a simple touch of hands, but Colton could swear he felt the same current from her. Rachel's eyes widened, and she glanced down at their joined hands, then pulled hers away. She didn't try to give back the quarter again, and he took that as a good sign.

"So, you're, ah, here with Luke and Mac? Is Jack still on his honeymoon?" she said as the waitress deposited a cup of coffee before her. Changing the subject, but still talking to him. Another good sign.

"Yes and yes. The three of us were grabbing breakfast." He glanced over his shoulder at his brothers. Luke arched a brow and shot him a grin. Mac was busy on his phone, probably working.

If Colton lived here, he'd probably see the three other Barlow boys a lot more often. That would be nice. Real nice.

As for his father...that was a work in progress. Somehow, Colton had had this crazy idea that everything would be good just because their first meeting went well. But his father hadn't been as warm and welcoming as his brothers had been, and Colton wasn't quite sure if he should continue to reach out or just let it go. Either way, it hurt, even if he was too damned old to care whether his daddy loved him.

Living here would mean seeing Bobby around town, too. That might not be such a benefit, given the rocky road they were on right now.

"As much as I complain about living in a circle and running into people I know everywhere I go, life here...grows on you," Rachel said, her voice soft and sweet. "It sounds like something from a Hallmark card, but living in a small town is like having a houseful of your favorite family and friends. They'll get on your nerves from time to time, but you're also so glad to see all those friendly faces whenever life gets tough." She ran a finger along the rim of her coffee cup, her eyes downcast, her voice even softer now. "When my mom died, it was the people of this town who helped me keep the shop running, and they've been the biggest supporters I could ask for. People keep trying to help my dad, too, but he's...stubborn."

Colton chuckled. "I think we all know someone like that. My mom is a stubborn woman, too. She…does things the way she wants to do them when she wants to do them." That was probably the nicest way he could say that his mother had been mostly consumed with her own life, leaving him and Katie to fend for themselves more often than not.

"You said you're their half brother. So you're not… Della's son?"

Even though Colton was old enough that he shouldn't care what people thought about how he was conceived, that didn't stop a little hesitation in his answer. He wondered if maybe Bobby was dealing with similar reactions to Colton's arrival. "No, I'm not. My father met my mother when he was working in Atlanta."

No need to divulge the family history that he had been the product of a brief affair. The Barlows were well loved in this town, and his conception had been more than thirty years ago. Ancient history that didn't need to be dragged forward. Colton was a man who much preferred to live in the present.

"How long have you known the rest of the Barlows?" Rachel asked.

"I just met them a couple weeks ago. I didn't know about any of them until now." He glanced over at Luke and Mac, who were grinning at him like a couple of fools. Clearly, there was going to be merciless teasing when he returned to the table. Which he should have done a long time ago, but he really liked talking to Rachel. Watching her smile, the way that gesture lit her eyes and brightened her face.

"Wow. That's a lot to digest in such a short time frame. No wonder you seemed a little…discombobulated when you came in the shop."

He chuckled. "Yeah, it's been a lot. But my brothers are great and that makes it easier."

"Well, you're in a good family. Mac, Luke and Jack are great guys."

It heartened him that his brothers were well liked. He wondered if maybe—by extension—Rachel would paint him with the same brush. "Does that approval umbrella extend over me, too?" Colton asked. "And encourage you to say yes when I remind you that I asked you out?"

She took a sip from the white mug, avoiding his gaze. "I thought I said no to a date."

"You were…vague. So let me try this again." He spun the stool until he was facing her head-on and looking into those deep green eyes. He knew he probably wasn't staying in this town for long. Knew he was crazy to date a woman he barely knew, a woman he wouldn't see again if he went back to Atlanta. But he wanted more of those smiles that seemed to light her from somewhere deep inside. "Would you like to go to dinner with me tonight, Rachel?"

She opened her mouth, closed it. "Tonight? As in this evening?"

He smirked. "That's usually the time people have dinner."

"It's just that I usually bring dinner to my dad's house and eat with him."

"Oh, okay. I understand." Disappointment weighed

in his gut. That no was a lot more definite. He laid a hand on the counter, inches away from hers, got to his feet. "Well, I'll let you enjoy your breakfast."

Just as he turned away, she covered his hand with her own. "But maybe I can meet you a little later. Like...seven?"

It was like he was fifteen again and the pretty girl in algebra had sent him a note across the aisle. He tried not to look like too much of an overeager dork. "Seven would be great. Let me pick you up. Make it an official date and everything."

"An official date?" She shook her head and let out a little laugh. "I haven't been on one of those in so long, I don't think I remember what to do."

"Just smile, Rachel," he said, reaching up and tracing an easy line along the curve of her smile. Wanting to do so much more than that. "The rest will fall right into place."

Just smile.

That was pretty much all she did the rest of the day. She smiled as she went over the bills. Smiled as she restocked the shelves. Smiled at Harvey when he came in with the daily bait delivery and smiled as she stacked containers of worms and crickets in the small refrigerator by the door.

The bell over the shop door rang a little after two, and Ginny Wilkins strode into the shop. Rachel had known Ginny pretty much all her life. The younger girl had been a cheerleader in high school and one of the most popular debutantes in all of Stone Gap. She came from a family that could trace its roots almost all the way to the Mayflower and had a six-acre property just on the edge of town, presided over by a two-story white antebellum mansion that had withstood hurricanes and the Civil War, and would probably outlast them all.

Ginny was also a girl known for extravagance in everything she did, which included the bright pink tea-length dress she was wearing, paired with an even brighter pink purse and flats. Her platinum-blond hair was done in bouncy curls that danced along her shoulders. "Rachel, I am so glad you are here!" Ginny said. "I need your help."

Rachel slid around the counter, a little perplexed as to why Ginny, the girliest girl she'd ever known, would be in a hardware shop. Maybe buying a gift for her father or boyfriend? "Sure. What do you need? We have a sale on—"

"I'm getting married!" The words exploded out of Ginny, complete with a little squeal and a wild flourish of a giant pear-shaped diamond on her left hand. "And I need you to plan it for me. I haven't the foggiest idea where to start or what to do."

"Ginny, I'm not doing that right now. I'm working here, at my dad's shop. I—"

"But you have to! You're the only one I trust. I mean, you did such a fabulous job with Arnelle Beauchamp's wedding and, oh, my, the venue you set up for Lucy Coleridge's wedding—amazing. I know you can do something even better for me. And that will make those two gooses green with envy over how amazing my wedding was." Ginny grinned. "You know there's nothing I like better than going further over the top than anyone else."

That was true. If there was one woman in Stone Gap to add more ruffles, more pink, more flowers, it was Ginny. She'd never been the kind to sit sedately in a corner. Everything she did, she did loud. Planning her wedding would be fun, Rachel thought. The kind of no-holds-barred event that would not only be an adventure, but also get people talking about Rachel's business.

The exact kind of jump-start she needed to get her company running again. If Ginny's wedding was a year or so away, there would be plenty of time for Rachel to both run the shop and get the event planned. And by then, surely her dad would be back at work every day.

Yes, she could make it work. Just thinking about getting back to the wedding-planning world that she loved caused a little tickle of excitement in Rachel's stomach. It was an incredible opportunity.

"I know the ideal location, Ginny. Perfect for the kind of wedding you want to have. There's this new hotel two towns away that's really something to talk about. It's pink and white and giant," Rachel said. She could already see it decorated in Ginny's signature color, imagine the band on the stage, the guests dining on something extravagant. It would be amazing, as Ginny had said.

"Pink? My favorite color!" Ginny exclaimed. The woman used more exclamation points in her daily speech than an Oscar winner. "All my bridesmaids are going to wear flamingo pink, and I'm going to have bright pink roses in my bouquet and a trail of them down the back of my dress, and it will look like I'm walking out of a garden. It's going to be all pink, all the time!"

Rachel bit back a grin at Ginny's ideas. That would be a wedding to remember for sure. "This hotel also has the most amazing outdoor patio, overlooking the water. You could have a gazebo on the patio and get married right there, with the boats in the background."

"Do you think we could get all the boats to have pink sails?" Ginny asked.

"I'm not sure," Rachel hedged. She could just see herself making that kind of request in the harbormaster's office. "That's a pretty tall order. But I'm sure we could hang pink organza from the gazebo and along the aisle."

Ginny clapped her hands. "Oh, my, that sounds too perfect for words! And do you think you can get it all done in three months?"

"Three…months?" A stone sank in Rachel's gut. "As in ninety days?"

"I know it's fast, but when you fall in love, you just don't want to wait. And I love my Bernard so very much." A smile stole across Ginny's face, the kind that only a woman truly in love wore, as if she had a secret no one else in the world possessed. It almost made Rachel jealous.

"There's no way I can get a wedding pulled together in three months," Rachel said, and tried not to let her own disappointment show through. This would have been the opportunity she'd needed, the big break that would breathe new life into her gasping business. "I'm still running this store full time. And the amount of work involved in such a short time frame…" She let out a long breath. "I'm sorry, Ginny."

"But you *have* to do it, Rachel. You are seriously the only one in the world I trust to handle my wedding. Can you please, pretty, pretty please, just think about it? Just for a day or two." Ginny cocked a hip to the side and wagged a pink-tipped nail in Rachel's direction. "You know, my wedding should make all the papers, and if my daddy has anything to say about it, it'll end up on the local news, too. That should be great for your business! A bonanza, for sure!"

It would be fantastic for her business. But Rachel couldn't see a way to make it work. There simply weren't enough hours in the day to do both. She couldn't let her father down, couldn't abandon his store. But instead of telling Ginny that straight out, Rachel found herself saying, "Yeah, sure, I'll think about it."

Ginny squealed, then drew Rachel into a tight hug. "Awesomesauce. I'll call you in a couple days or you call me. I'm so excited!"

After waving as Ginny pulled away from the curb in her pink Mercedes, Rachel let her smile falter as she slowly walked back into the empty shop. There were no customers, and the full shelves and almost empty cash register seemed to mock her. She was spending her days here, trying to keep her father's dream alive, while her own died a slow death.

On the back wall hung a series of plaques and a small shelf of trophies. Best Fisherman, Biggest Catch, Good Neighbor Award. All the things that made up her

dad and his life here in Stone Gap. It was like walking through her memories, remembering the fishing
trips to the lake, perched in the back of the boat when
he reeled in the biggest bass anyone had ever seen, sitting on a hard metal folding chair in the lobby of the
town hall while the mayor of Stone Gap handed her
father a plaque and a citation for his help the day after
a hurricane whipped through Stone Gap and leveled
half the town.

That was the kind of guy her dad was. Hard-working,
competitive, considerate to his neighbors, to everyone
who knew him. She couldn't abandon him.

Couldn't put his dreams on the shelf while she went
after her own. Even if a part of her heart broke as she
thought about letting her dream flutter away in a cloud
of pink.

Chapter Four

Colton had never been the kind of guy that anyone would describe as romantic. He didn't remember Valentine's Day, rarely thought to bring flowers and stumbled over his words whenever he tried to say something poetic.

Yet here he stood in the Garden of Eden flower shop in downtown Stone Gap a little after six in the evening, debating between roses and lilies. They all looked the same to him, a jumble of pinks and yellows and reds, and he realized he didn't know enough about Rachel to tell which she liked best.

God, this was a stupid idea. He could buy the wrong kind of flowers, or buy too many and make her wonder about his intentions. Maybe he should have picked up one of those solitary roses in the bucket on the counter at the gas station. Or nothing at all. Colton started to turn and leave when a familiar figure walked into the shop.

His younger brother Luke. A very, very welcome sight.

"If you ask me, roses are overrated. Women like something creative," Luke said. He slipped into place beside Colton, the two of them squaring off against the colorful refrigerator case like two gunfighters. "Something that tells them you thought it through, or at least made a stab at thinking."

"Does staring at all these options for twenty minutes, too damned confused to pick anything out, count?"

Luke chuckled. "Nope. Sorry." He gestured toward the refrigerated case stuffed with fresh flowers. In the background, a saleslady in a green apron hovered, ready to jump in at any time. She'd already offered her help three times, but Colton had thought he could do this on his own.

Ha-ha. Yeah, he pretty much sucked at this romance thing.

"So," Luke said, "I take it the agonizing over flowers is part of your campaign to impress the beautiful and intriguing Rachel Morris?"

Even though his brothers had teased him when he'd returned to their table in the diner that morning, he hadn't told them he had asked Rachel out. He'd just changed the subject when the food arrived, and the two of them had let it drop. Colton thought maybe his conversation with Rachel—and his interest in her—

had dropped below Luke and Mac's radar. Yeah, not so much. "How did you know that?"

"For one, you ditched us to talk to her—"

"Sorry." Luke was right. The time he had with his brothers was limited, and he should have stayed at the table instead of getting distracted so easily.

"No need to apologize. Pretty women always take precedence. Though you should expect some serious teasing in the days ahead." Luke grinned. "All part of the initiation."

"There's an initiation?"

"Of course. You didn't expect us to just let you become a Barlow without one, did you?"

Colton chuckled. "Guess not." Then he glanced over at his brother, half his flesh and blood. When it came to his brothers, Colton already felt like he was part of the family. With his father…not so much. "Though I don't think it's quite that simple."

"You talking about Dad?" Luke let out a sigh. "I don't think it's anything personal. I think he's just struggling with the whole thing. You being here, what that means in…"

"In what?" Colton prompted.

"In a town this size. People talk, you know, and most people talk more than they should. About crap they know nothing about."

That was what Colton had been afraid of. That even at his age, being an illegitimate son was mostly an embarrassment. What had he been thinking, just showing up here last week? At Jack's wedding, at that?

His uncle Tank had warned him that Bobby might

be...difficult. *It's going to take some getting used to*, Tank had said. *My brother isn't one to embrace change. He's a stick who is very happy staying in the mud.*

Maybe this was how his relationship with Bobby would be going forward. Was that enough for Colton? If it never progressed beyond small talk and awkward pauses?

"Maybe it would be best if I went back to Atlanta," he said.

Luke scoffed. "Best for who? Not for me and Mac. Not for you. And not for Dad. I love my—our—dad, don't get me wrong, but he's being an ass." He put up a hand before Colton could argue. "Now, back to the top priority. The pretty woman. You need swoon-worthy flowers, and I need flowers that say, *forgive me for being a Neanderthal.*"

Colton smirked. "They sell those here?"

Luke laughed. "They better. Or I'm in trouble again tonight."

"What'd you do?"

"I had a fight with Peyton." Luke threw up his hands. "I know, I know. But in my defense, it was a busy day and I was a little tired. And missed lunch."

Colton chuckled. Even he knew an empty stomach wasn't grounds for an argument with your fiancée. Luke was smart to be buying flowers.

"I don't even know what to tell you."

"Just help me pick out some flowers that say, *I'm sorry I was an idiot.*" A sheepish grin filled Luke's face. "I love Peyton too much to argue with her for more than five seconds. All I want to do is see her smile again."

At the mention of the word, a slow smile curved across Luke's face. Colton envied that look. That pure…joy on his brother's face when he talked about the woman he loved. Colton had never felt that way about anyone before. Had come close a few times, but never opened his whole heart like his brothers had with the women they clearly adored.

"Now, for you," Luke said, "I recommend the almost-deluxe bouquet. You get a little of this, a little of that, not so many you're walking in there with a garden in your hands, but enough to say, *Hey, I like you.* An almost-deluxe bouquet is not so fancy that it screams *trying too hard* and not so casual that it says *yanked off the highway median at the last second.*" Luke put up his hands. "Been there, done that. The results were… unsatisfactory."

Colton laughed. "I'll keep that in mind."

In the end, he settled on a midsize bouquet with white and yellow daisies, a few pink lilies and a bunch of dark purple flowers he didn't recognize. The saleslady wrapped it in thick paper, giving him all kinds of instructions about water and trimming the stems and something about a packet of floral preservative that she tucked between the stems. He just nodded and said yes to everything. Luke did the same, and a few minutes later the two of them were standing on the sidewalk.

"Good Lord. We look like Cupid's minions," Luke said.

Colton chuckled. "Might have to turn in our man cards."

"It's all worth it, big brother, when she smiles that sweet smile of hers and says your name." Luke clapped him on the shoulder. "Now I better get out of here before we both need some Kleenex."

Colton watched his brother walk away, Luke's steps light and his smile wise. Colton never had been a romantic guy, but maybe it was time to change his ways—if doing so meant having the kind of happiness that hung around Luke like a ray of sunshine.

"You're fidgety this evening," her father said. He set his crossword puzzle to the side and laced his fingers together. "What's going on?"

"I…ah, just had too much coffee today." If she told her father she had a date, there'd be all kinds of questions. She wasn't sure this thing with Colton would go anywhere past an appetizer, so better not to say anything at all. It was just a dinner, nothing more.

Her father peered at her over the bridge of his reading glasses. "And that's why you're wearing a new dress? And fancy shoes?"

"How did you—"

He leaned across the table then reached around her neck and pulled up a tag. "You forgot something."

That was what she got for being in a rush today and buying the dress in the few minutes she had between leaving the shop and going to her dad's. It was a wonder she'd made it out of the store at all, given how nervous and rushed she'd been. Rachel scrambled to her feet and fished the scissors out of the junk drawer. She reached over her shoulder but couldn't quite grasp the small tag. Her father got to his feet, crossed to her, lifted the tag then took the scissors from her hands. "Let me do that for you," he said. "You've done more than enough for me."

"Thanks, Dad."

He pressed the small price tag into her palm. "You're welcome." Then his pale blue eyes met hers and his gaze softened. "I'm sorry."

"Sorry? For what?"

"For taking up every minute of your life with my... inertia." He waved at the cluttered kitchen table, the dirty dishes in the sink, the pile of clean laundry waiting to be put away. "You deserve your own life. I'm glad you're going out tonight. You don't need to spend every night here, taking care of a tired old man."

She cupped his cheek, settling her palm against the rough stubble of his unshaven beard. "For the record, you are neither tired nor old. And I enjoy spending time with you."

His smile turned bittersweet and his eyes shone with unshed tears. "Get out of here. Go on your date. I'll be fine."

"But what about dinner and—"

"I know how to make a peanut butter sandwich. I'll be fine."

She thought of all the meals her father had skipped. All the times he'd fallen asleep in this very kitchen chair, forgotten to take his daily heart medication... there were a thousand things he hadn't done, a million ways he hadn't been fine. "I should stay..."

"You should go." He waved her toward the door. "I mean it."

She started to argue again, but saw the determination in her father's eyes. Maybe he was feeling better, and maybe he was going to start being more independent. Doubts clouded her thoughts, but in the end, she relented. "Okay, but if you need anything—"

"I know how to dial a phone." Her father smiled. It was a dimmer-watt smile than the one she knew and loved, but nevertheless, it was a start. "Have a good time, sweetheart."

She nearly turned back toward her dad's house three times on her way to her apartment. Picked up her phone twice at a stop sign to call and check on him. She pulled under the carport, parked then stared at the phone in her hand and debated. He had said he would be okay. If she hovered too much, he'd never move forward. But if she didn't hover enough...

Surely her dad would be okay for a few hours. Besides, this date could be over before dessert. She might not like that hot single firefighter with the crooked smile.

Uh-huh. That was a likely scenario.

If she didn't finish getting ready, he'd find her outside her apartment half assembled. Not that she probably wouldn't look like that, anyway. Rachel was the complete opposite of a girlie-girl. She was happier in jeans than heels, and more comfortable in a faded T-shirt than a fancy dress.

She turned off the car then headed inside. She had

ten minutes until Colton arrived. Just enough time to check her makeup and hair for the thirtieth time.

Just as she was about to dial her father's number, Rachel's cell rang. Melissa's smiling face popped up on the caller ID. "Before you ask," Rachel said when she answered the call, a knowing laugh in her voice, "yes, I did go with the black heels."

"Those strappy ones with the silver buckle?"

"The very ones." Melissa had been the first one Rachel had called after she'd agreed to the date with Colton. Her friend had cast the deciding vote among the three dresses Rachel had found in a little shop downtown between work and her dad's. She'd been the one to talk Rachel into a pair of shoes she never expected to wear again, though she had to admit they looked really cute. "My feet have totally forgotten what it feels like to wear heels, and I think they're going to stage a coup very soon."

Melissa laughed. "If you're lucky, the heels won't be on for long."

"It's just dinner," Rachel said, reminding herself as much as Melissa.

"Who says you can't have an appetizer first? Or dessert after?" Melissa let out a throaty laugh. "Preferably both, if you get lucky."

The thought of ending up in bed with Colton sent electricity through her veins. A man like that, with a rock-hard body and a ready smile, was the kind who would leave her breathless at the end of the night. And it had been so long—way too long—since she'd been with anyone that just the mere thought of curling around him in her queen-size bed was almost too much. "I hardly know the man."

"Trust me, that's a good thing. Once you know them well, they start leaving their socks on the floor and belching at the dinner table. Better to go with a stranger who at least has a semblance of manners. And mystery."

"You love Jason." Rachel had always envied Melissa and Jason's marriage. They still shared secret smiles and private jokes, and nearly every opportunity they got they were either holding hands or leaving a little touch on the other's shoulder. It was a nice relationship, the kind Rachel dreamed of having for herself someday. When she had more than a couple hours on a weekday evening to devote to dating.

"I do love my husband. I just don't love all his manness." Melissa laughed. "Who am I kidding? Of course I do. But sometimes I wish he would go back to being the guy I dated. The one who tried so hard to impress me with his chivalry that he broke a toe opening the door to The Chalet restaurant too fast."

Rachel laughed. "I remember that. And then he spent the rest of the night trying to pretend it didn't hurt."

"Until I insisted on taking him to the emergency room, and spending our first date between a guy who had been stabbed in the thigh and a woman with the flu. Hold on a sec." Melissa's voice moved farther from the phone. "Jason, Jr., you cannot feed your little sister your peas. And no, you can't give them to the dog, either." She came back to the phone with a sigh. "Want some kids? Free of charge."

"Not tonight, but I promise to babysit Friday night so you and Jason can get a night out. Maybe *you'll* get lucky," Rachel said.

"Right now my version of getting lucky is him remembering to see if I'm in the car before he pulls away," Melissa laughed. "Anyway, have a great time tonight with that hunk of burning love. And don't disappoint me by being home before midnight."

Rachel said goodbye then peeked in the mirror yet again. She debated the dress and shoes for the thirtieth time—too much? Too fancy? Too sexy?—then decided if she changed, Melissa would never let her hear the end of it. Then the doorbell rang, which meant she was out of time to stall.

She let out a deep breath then pulled open the door. "Hi."

Colton smiled. It was the kind of smile that washed over her and sent a little thrill through her veins. "Hi yourself. You look…amazing."

Just to see that look in his eyes made the purchase a total win. Her gaze took in the rest of him, the clean-shaven chin, the pale blue button-down shirt open at his neck, the dress pants that outlined a very trim, very nice, body. The conversation with Melissa— and Rachel's fantasy about ending up in her bed with Colton—rushed back to her mind, complete with images of unbuttoning his shirt, and tugging those pants down his legs. Good Lord. She was going to have to start fanning herself any second. "Thank you. I'm not normally dressed up like this," she said, waving a hand over the outfit. "I feel like a fish in an evening gown."

He chuckled. "I'd say more like a mermaid. You are beautiful, no matter what you wear."

She blushed, a burst of crimson that filled her cheeks and trailed down the V-neck of her dress. He decided he should make her blush more often. "Thank you again. You look great, too."

"Oh, these are for you." He thrust a bouquet of flowers at her.

White and yellow daisies, pink stargazer lilies, long stalks of purple lavender peppered with stems of baby's breath, all wrapped in a thick paper cone. It was a sweet bouquet, one that went beyond the cliché of roses. She wondered what sort of meaning he attached to their date as she caught the heady scent of the lilies.

He seemed nervous, which made her smile. Maybe she wasn't the only one who hadn't been on a date in a while. She brought the flowers to her nose and inhaled. "They're gorgeous. Thank you."

"You're welcome." He gestured toward his car. "Should we go?"

"Let me put these in water first." She glanced back at him. "Do you want to come in for a minute?"

As soon as he entered her apartment, the space felt too small, too confined. He was six feet two inches of brawny man, with his smile and his big blue eyes that reminded her of the ocean on a sunny day. Nerves fluttered in her gut, which was crazy. She never got nervous, never got flustered around guys. Or at least she never had—

Until she'd met Colton Barlow.

Now the man had her thoughts running in twelve different directions, half of which led straight to her bedroom. The nine hundred square feet she lived in made that bed seem awfully close. Too close. Too tempting.

She reached for a vase above the fridge, and her silly nervous hands nearly dropped it. Colton was there, right behind her, his body so close to hers, all she'd have to do was inhale and she'd be pressed against him.

"Let me get that," he said, his voice deep beside her ear.

"Thanks." She knew she should step away, but she stayed where she was, in the few inches of space between Colton's chest and her refrigerator. He grasped the vase and brought it down to her in one slow, liquid movement. She took it with one hand then turned to look up at him.

Her heart beat. Her breath flowed in, out. And her gaze locked on his, on the ocean depths that seemed to darken as one second passed, then another, another. "Thank...thank you."

"My pleasure."

The word *pleasure* sent heat spiraling through her. How far away was her bedroom? Twenty feet? Thirty?

God, what was wrong with her? She couldn't haul the man off to her room before they even had a date. She started to step to the side, but Colton moved at the same time, and they collided, chest to chest. Heat erupted inside her, a deep, yawning want that nearly took her breath away. She looked up at him, the vase forgotten, the flowers a distant memory.

And held her breath.

Slowly, oh, so slowly, Colton brought his face down to hers. His eyes never wavered from her gaze, and she thought a girl could get lost in that sea. His fingers danced along her cheek, trailed down to her jaw, skipped over her lips. She opened her mouth—to protest, to agree, she wasn't sure—and then his lips were on hers, and she was lost.

His kiss started slow, sweet and easy, like sliding into a warm pool on a cool day. He shifted against her, and she reached up, gliding her hands along the cotton of his shirt, inching over the ridged muscles of his back.

He deepened the kiss, the two of them moving in concert now, her mouth opening to his, his tongue darting in. She let out a little mew and arched into him, wanting, needing, seeking more.

His fingers tangled in her hair, and she swore he whispered her name against her lips before his tongue swept in and urged hers to dance. He was hard against her, and she pressed into him, wanting more, wanting... *everything*. He felt so good, so right.

He brought his hand down to her cheek again, a tender, sweet touch, then he shifted back, away from her. The kiss ended, but he hovered there, just inches from her face. "This is going to go...somewhere it shouldn't, very fast. We should go to dinner before..."

Before they ended up in her bedroom. A part of her wanted to say, *But I want it to go there. I want it to go twenty feet down the hall, to that queen-size mattress and those crisp white sheets.*

Then her sanity returned, and she nodded. "You're right. Let's go." She started to reach for her purse on the counter.

He touched her hand, drew her back. "The flowers?"

"Flowers?" she repeated, confused.

A grin quirked up one side of his face. "Remember? The vase that started all this?"

Her face heated. "Oh, yes. I just…forgot."

Got totally distracted by he-of-the-blue-eyes-and-incredible-kissing-ability, was more like it. She spun away, grabbed the vase and busied herself with filling it then trimming the stems and dropping the bouquet into the glass container. She set it on the window ledge over her sink then left the light on above them. Not that the flowers would know or care, but when she came home tonight, it would be nice to see the flowers there.

Nice because they would remind her of the way this night had started. And if that was any indication of what lay ahead, she was already happy she'd agreed to go out with Colton Barlow.

Chapter Five

His dinner at the Sea Shanty could have been cardboard, for all Colton noticed.

All of his attention was focused on the intriguing, beautiful woman across from him. A woman he had kissed—and who had made something as simple as that seem like the most incredible experience he'd had in a long, long time.

In her elegant black dress and heels, she was as feminine as a debutante, but then she got talking about baseball, and she could have been one of the guys. Except he never looked at the chest of one of the guys and fantasized about trailing kisses down the valley between their breasts.

"When Henderson stole third in that Yankees game back in '85, he was incredible to watch, though I didn't see it live, just on a replay of old games I watched with my dad. Every Saturday we watched those classic games, and Henderson was his favorite player," she said. "No one mastered the art of the stolen base like Henderson did."

"He had, what, eighty steals that season?" Colton said. "He was like David Copperfield out there."

She took a sip of her wine. "In '83, he stole one hundred bases in one season. No one's done that, before or since. Amazing stuff."

Colton buttered a slice of ciabatta and set it on the edge of his plate. "I don't think I've ever met a woman who knows as much about baseball as you do."

She shrugged. "Only child syndrome. My dad wasn't into playing with dolls, so we bonded over baseball. He taught me how to play, and we watched tons of games together. One year we even took a trip to Louisville to visit the slugger museum. I still have the bat he bought me and had engraved with my name." A sad smile stole over her face. "I miss those days with my dad. Ever since my mom died, he hasn't wanted to go to a game, or sit through one on TV. Never mind do anything else he used to do. It's like he just stopped living."

"That's got to be hard for you."

She shrugged again, but he could see the stress in her face, the burden on her shoulders. "He's my dad. I'm going to support him however I can."

"But you have a right to a life, too."

She waved that off. "It can wait. He needs me now."

Yet another reason to like Rachel. She was the kind of woman who did the right thing, who stuck by her family when they needed her. He'd known far too many women—which probably went back to his bad choosing skills—who were more interested in the label on their back than the people in their life. Rachel's lack of self-centeredness certainly made her stand out.

Colton thought about his sister and his mother. For nearly all his life, he had been the one taking care of them. Making sure his little sister got up for school and took a lunch with her. Making sure the house doors were locked tight for the night after his mother got home from work. Making sure there was gas in the car, the trash put out on the curb, a little more money in the bank. Katie was an adult now, living on her own and highly successful at the accounting firm where she worked, while his mother was still flitting from job to job, living arrangement to living arrangement. He'd only been gone for a few days, but he still worried about them.

"I understand putting family first," he said. "I guess I always felt it was my responsibility to take care of my mom and sister. I was the only man in the house, know what I mean?"

"Even when you were little? Because you didn't have your dad then?"

Colton wondered how his life would have been different if his father had been involved from the start. Uncle Tank had been great, a regular presence at the house, but it hadn't been the same as having a full-time dad. His brothers had turned into great men, as far as Colton could tell, which meant their father must have had a good influence.

"It just seemed like the right thing to do. To take care of them, to protect them," Colton said. "I don't know, maybe it's an instinct for men."

"Not all men." She shook her head, and a smile filled her face. "You're pretty incredible, you know that? Helping to take care of your mother and sister, then becoming a firefighter, where you rescue people from burning buildings for a living? You're like a hero."

He cut his gaze away. The cozy restaurant suddenly seemed ten times smaller. In his head he could hear Willis and Foster, hear their shouts grow in pitch and volume as concern turned to worry, turned to panic. And Colton, trying so hard to get past the wall of burning timbers, trying to climb in there and grab a hand, a foot, anything. But then the ceiling came down in a shower of sparks and wood, and then the screams stopped—

"Colton?"

Rachel's soft voice drew him back. He shifted in his seat and picked up the bread, swirling it in the sauce. "Sorry. My mind...wandered."

"Okay." She fiddled with her wineglass, and he could tell she knew he was keeping something from her.

But how could he tell her that he had watched two of his friends die? That the man she thought was a hero was still paying the price for what had happened, was still carrying the weight of his own guilt?

What he needed to do was change the subject, swing them back around to the fun conversation they'd been having earlier tonight. Because as much as he told himself he shouldn't get any more involved with a woman he was probably never going to see again, Colton craved more of her smile, more of her voice, more of everything. More of her.

Tomorrow would take care of itself. For now he had tonight, and an intriguing, beautiful woman sitting across from him.

"You know, you still owe me the twenty-five-cent tour of Stone Gap," he said as the waitress took their empty plates away. "And I think we should start at the Good Eatin' Café, because I hear they have the best apple pie in the county, and all the Sea Shanty is offering tonight is cheesecake. I don't know about you, but I'm a pie guy."

She laughed. "They do, indeed. And the best pecan pie in the world. I'd eat it every day, if I could."

That had him suddenly craving pie in the worst way. "Then let's get out of here and go get some pie."

She nodded. "I think that sounds like a great idea. Though I have to warn you, after that, there's not a lot to see."

His gaze raked over the woman before him, with her dancing green eyes and warm, welcoming smile. "I think there's a lot worth seeing in this town."

Rachel was trying really hard not to like Colton Barlow.

She had her life all mapped out, her days planned to the last minute, and falling for a guy like Colton made her want to ditch those plans. Even tonight she was ignoring the books for the store, and the orders she should be placing, to run around town in his rental car with the windows down and the breeze in her hair.

But it felt so good to be doing something so…relaxing. No bills to worry about paying, no sales to worry about increasing, nothing but just being in the car with a sexy man who was interested in her. She'd worry about tomorrow later. For now there was only Colton.

They stopped in at the Good Eatin' Café first, where Viv rushed right over and seated them in a booth. "Oh, I'm so glad to see you, Rachel, and out with a handsome gentleman, too."

Rachel flushed and decided the best course of action was to ignore Viv's comment. "What kind of pies do you have tonight?"

"Apple, pecan and a strawberry rhubarb."

Rachel glanced at Colton. He nodded. "How about a slice of each?" she said.

"Coming right up. Extra whipped cream?" Viv asked.

"Definitely," Colton said.

When Viv was gone, Rachel crossed her hands on the table and smiled at Colton. "We had the same exact thought."

"We both know a good pie, or rather pies, when we hear it." He grinned.

Viv brought the pies a second later, along with two cups of decaf and a pair of forks. "Enjoy, kids."

"Thank you, Viv." Rachel picked up her fork, then cut off a piece of the pecan. "Here, taste this first, because it's a pie to measure all others against, believe me."

"If I was a gentleman, I'd insist you take the first bite, but…" He leaned forward and took the bite.

Rachel could hardly concentrate. There was a dollop of whipped cream on Colton's lip, and she was dying to lean across the table and kiss it off. "You…you have a little…" She rose in her seat, closed the distance between them and instead of kissing it or licking it, she swiped the whipped cream off his lip with her finger.

Before she could sit down again, he grabbed her hand and gently licked the little bit of whipped cream off her finger. Her hormones sent up a loud cheer, and her gut tightened. "Thank you," Colton said.

"You're…welcome." She could barely eat her slice of pie, because every time she glanced at the dessert, she thought about the whipped cream on Colton's lip, and the sexy way he'd…

Stop, Rachel. Just don't go there.

Too soon—or maybe not soon enough—they had finished the pie and were heading back out to his car.

She was going to concentrate on showing him around Stone Gap. Not the thought of climbing in her backseat with a canister of whipped cream—

No. That wasn't a productive thought. At all.

"Now this isn't going to be your ordinary tour," she said. "We're going to start with the haunted house. And if you're still hungry later on, we can move on to some cookies from Betty's Bakery and then possibly some beach time. There's nothing like walking on the beach when it's dark and all you have for light is the moon."

"So, what's the theme of the twenty-five-cent tour?"

"All you can see for twenty-five cents worth of gas."

"That's not going to get us far."

"It's a small town." She grinned and pointed to the street ahead of them. "Take a left here then your first right."

He did as she instructed, and a moment later they pulled in front of a dilapidated mansion. Once, it had been amazing—Rachel had seen photos of it in a book in the library—but those days were long past. The front of the house stood tall and erect, as if it was putting on a brave front against the powers of the ocean winds at the back. The white paint had grayed and peeled, the expansive wraparound porch leaned into the back of the house, collapsed onto itself. Most of the windows were broken, the shutters hanging askew, and the landscaping was so overgrown it almost blocked the first floor from view. "Rumor has it that Gareth Richardson killed his family in this house," Rachel said, "and he still walks the floors at night, moaning his regrets."

"Should we go inside?" Colton asked. "Go pay Gareth a visit?"

She laughed. "I don't think it's safe, but…"

Colton was already out of the car and coming around to her side. He opened her door and put out a hand. "You're with me, remember? I'll keep you safe."

She slid her hand into his warm, firm grip. She wanted to ask if he would keep her heart safe, too, but it was way too early to ask or even think that. But as she looked up into his grin and felt the warmth of his touch on hers, Rachel realized she was already falling hard for the firefighter from Atlanta.

They picked their way through the overgrown yard, using the light from Colton's phone as a guide, then he led her up the three stairs of the porch and nudged at the front door. It opened with a lonely creak, into a dark, yawning cavern of a house. A few dots of moonlight speckled the old wood floors.

"Already looks spooky," Colton whispered.

"It does. Really spooky." She gripped his arm. "Maybe I should hold on. In case, you know…the ghost comes out."

"Definitely a good idea," he said and drew her tight against his body.

The scent of his cologne—warm, spicy, dark—filled the space between them. She could feel his heart beneath her palm, imagine the ripples of his muscles under his shirt. She barely noticed the dark or the house or the spooky rooms they explored. She noticed only him, the feel of him and how that made her want Colton more with each passing second.

Her mind kept going back to his kiss. The way he had touched her cheek, made her feel inordinately special. It was exciting and heady and tempting. Maybe too tempting.

They stopped in the kitchen. A shaft of moonlight poured in through the broken kitchen window, illuminating scarred wooden floors and floral wallpaper hanging in sheets. The center of the ceiling bulged above them, as if it were about to open up at any moment.

"This would be a cool house to restore," Colton said. "It would make a cool bed-and-breakfast, too."

She scoffed. "It's way beyond restoration. You're better off tearing it down and building new."

"Maybe so. But then you'd lose the history. And the little quirks that make this house what it is. I like history. Maybe because I only knew half of mine growing up."

"And now you have a chance to know the other half."

"I'm trying," he said. "But my father hasn't been very open to it. Luke thinks it's because it's hard for my father to deal with the stares and gossip."

"That's the downside to living in a small town. I can understand that." How many times had she seen people whisper then shake their heads and look away when she had been a little girl? The rumors about her mother had been constant whispers in the background. She could understand how tough this was for Colton, for Bobby. Stone Gap could wrap around you like a warm blanket, but it could also be a cold, lonely place to live when there were secrets to keep, or people to protect.

Rachel shook her head. Maybe it was the dark rooms, or the fact that Colton still had his arm around her, but she suddenly felt vulnerable and scared.

You'll be safe, he'd said. Did he mean the same thing if she opened up to him, if she told this man—who was, after all, practically a stranger still—all the guilty feelings and regrets that crowded on her shoulders every day? The emotional burdens that kept her rooted firmly in that little hardware store?

"I can understand that because when I was growing up my mom was an alcoholic," she said quietly. "And people talked. They saw her driving when she shouldn't have been behind the wheel or heard her crazy outbursts at a school play, and there'd be talk. And those looks of…pity for me. Because I was her daughter."

Colton turned until she was in his arms, and her gaze had lifted to his. In the moonlight, he seemed taller, stronger, broader. "That's tough," he said. "I can't even imagine how hard that would be. No wonder you're such a tough cookie, Rachel Morris."

His soft words of admiration warmed her. Maybe this man, who was also in that awful club of being the one the townspeople whispered about, could understand her. "It's why I'm so close to my dad. It's like we formed this little team. When my mom was sober, everything was perfect and wonderful. Like a regular family. But other times…" She shrugged.

"I get it. I used to pretend my uncle was my real father. He was just a family friend, as far as I knew, but there were times when he would be over at my house, and I'd pretend that I was his son. I just wanted a father so bad, like the rest of my friends… But whenever he left, it was just me and my mom and my sister. We were a little team, just like you had with your dad, but—"

"It wasn't the same," she cut in, finishing his thought. "I guess we have more in common than just a love of baseball," she said, because right now, she felt too close to him, too close to falling over some crazy edge.

"I think we have more than that in common," he

said, his voice low and dark in the dim space. He shifted closer, then raised his hand to trail along her jaw.

Hot anticipation pooled inside her. It felt like Christmas and her birthday and the first day of spring all rolled together and dipped in chocolate.

Colton leaned in, hovered over her lips for a heartbeat. "I want to kiss you again."

"And I want you to kiss me."

"If we do this," he said, moving closer until his words danced across her mouth, "it might change things. One kiss can be an accident. Two is…more."

She drew in a breath. "Do you want more?"

"I don't know," he said, but his gaze never left hers, those blue eyes looking like dark pools.

"That's okay," she whispered, "because I don't know, either."

She saw the flash of his smile, then he kissed her. This one was faster, harder, more insistent than the first. The kind of kiss that ignited her veins, had her surging into him, made her wonder if there was a floor in this house sturdy enough to make love on. His hands roamed down the silky fabric of her dress, sliding down her back, over the curve of her buttocks, lingering at her waist, then down again.

It was sweet, it was hot, it was one of the best kisses she'd ever had. And she never wanted it to end. But then the wind started up outside, and the house began to creak, and Colton drew back. "I think old Gareth is making his presence known. Maybe we should get out of here."

"There's still some things to see on the tour," she said.

"I can't wait." He grinned, then he took her hand and they darted out of the house just as the walls began to shiver and the wind kicked up, blowing leaves and branches around in the yard.

A wicked storm moved in as they got in the car, canceling the rest of the tour. The rain hit the windshield faster than the wipers could keep up, and Colton drove her back at a snail's pace. It wasn't until they pulled up in front of her building that Rachel glanced at the time.

Nearly eleven. She'd spent four hours with this man, and it had passed as quickly as four minutes. She wanted more, but it would all have to wait.

Turning to say good-night, she suddenly felt shy. "I…I have to go. I have work to do before I go to bed."

He ran a finger along her cheek, and she resisted the almost overpowering urge to lean into his touch. Because she knew if she did, she'd kiss him again, and then she'd never get out of this car. Never get back to the responsibilities she had temporarily ignored. "What are you doing tomorrow night?"

She caught his finger in her palm. "I don't have time in my life for this, Colton."

"Neither do I. So let's just have one more date and then call it quits."

She couldn't help but laugh. "Seriously?"

"One more date, Rachel."

She smirked. "One. No more."

"Nope. Because I'm sure you will figure out after one more date with me that I'm not such a good catch, after all. That I have numerous bad habits…"

"Name one."

He pretended to think it over. "I hate doing the dishes. I'd rather eat out of a take-out container than wash a plate."

She laughed again. When had she laughed this much? With anyone? It was so wonderful, so energizing, so addictive. "That's why God invented dishwashers."

"And I can't dance. What kind of Southern man can't dance?"

"One who lets the girl lead," she said then pressed a quick kiss to his lips and dashed out of the car before she was tempted to stay much, much longer.

Chapter Six

Bobby Barlow stared at his two sons, who were standing in his kitchen with their arms crossed over their chests. They'd shown up at the house late this afternoon, ostensibly to say hello to their mother, but after Della left for bridge with the girls, Luke and Mac had stayed behind and given him the silent treatment staredown. "What?"

"You need to see Colton," Luke said. "He's only in town for a few days."

"I did see Colton." Bobby scowled. "At Jack's wedding, and I ran into him at the Sea Shanty the other night."

Well, ran into him but barely talked to him. He had seen the disappointment on Colton's face, the disapproval on Della's face and still sat there at the table with Jerry and Stella Norton and talked about the Steelers' chances of making it to the Super Bowl. The whole way home, Della had given him The Eye—the one that said she wasn't pleased with what he had done, but wasn't going to say anything. She didn't have to. He'd been married to her for nearly thirty-five years, and he knew when she was mad, and what she was mad about.

This time, it was him. And his struggle with making his fourth son part of the family.

"Family dinner is on Sunday, and I think he's staying in town at least through the weekend," Mac said. "Invite Colton."

"So we can tease him," Luke added. "And so somebody else can do the dishes afterward."

"Great idea," Mac whispered to his brother. "Maybe we'll even tell him it's customary for him to bring dessert."

"And a case of beer." Luke grinned.

Bobby put up his hands. He had to admire his boys for being so stubborn. He wanted to ask where they got that from, but all he had to do was look in the mirror. After all, his mother had always told him to be careful or his kids would turn out just like him. They were—but a better, stronger version of himself. "All right, all right. I'll call him. You two don't have to badger me about it."

"Yeah, we do, Dad." Mac dropped into one of the kitchen chairs. "Listen, we get that it's hard to explain where Colton came from—"

"And the fact that you can't say the stork dropped

him off on the doorstep, because that would have to be one hell of a big stork," Luke added.

"But he's a good guy," Mac went on. "And he's part of this family now, so everyone needs to treat him as such."

Bobby pulled three beers out of the fridge and tossed two to his sons. He unscrewed the cap, then sent it sailing into the trash. "It's not that easy."

"What's not easy? You say, 'This is Colton, he's my son,' end of subject." Mac spun the beer between his palms and kept his gaze on the bottle. "People make mistakes, Dad. Your friends are going to understand that. Plus, it was more than thirty years ago."

Bobby shook his head. "That's not it."

"Are you embarrassed by having Colton here?" Luke said. "Because he's a good guy, Dad, and you need to get over that."

Bobby could see his other two sons liked their half brother, and were ready to do whatever it took to include him in the family. They were good kids, he realized, kids that he had helped raise. Though most of the credit should go to Della, because she was the one who had kept this family running when he was busy with the shop or doing the rest of his own growing up—being that Bobby was a man like many other men, who took their sweet time settling into marriage. Without his wife, he knew he wouldn't have been half the man he'd turned out to be, and wouldn't have half the incredible family he had.

"I'm not embarrassed by Colton's presence," Bobby said. "I mean, yeah, I have to do some explaining to folks, but hell, at my age, I don't give a rat's ass if people like me or not. That's not why I'm hesitating."

Luke leaned against the fridge and crossed his arms over his chest. "Then what is it?"

Bobby sighed and ran a hand through his head. One thing about Colton appearing in his life—it was forcing him to open up. For a man who rarely talked about anything more emotional than the crushing defeat of his favorite football team, this stuff was hard. "It's your mother."

"What? Mom is fine with Colton. She's been warmer than you to him, in fact." Mac shook his head. "Don't blame this on her."

"I'm not." Bobby took a swig of the beer but it didn't do anything except delay the next sentence. He wasn't going to tell the boys about how distant Della had been the last few days. How it seemed there was something on her mind, and how he'd avoided asking about it because he was pretty sure the topic would include the words *affair, betrayal, child*. He loved his wife, and if there was one thing he regretted, it was how much all of this had hurt the amazing woman who had stuck by him, even when he was being a total moron. But here she was, paying the price right alongside him. "I'm trying to keep this whole thing with Colton under wraps because I don't want people to look badly at your mother."

"Why would they do that?" Luke asked. Then he thought a second. "Oh…because she stayed with you through all this."

"Yeah." Bobby let out a sigh. He should have dealt

with this years ago, so that it wouldn't have the impact it was having now. Della deserved better than that. She probably deserved better than him, better than how casually he had treated their marriage in the early years. "People in this town love your mother. I don't want anyone to look at her sideways because of a mistake I made."

"They won't, Dad, if you lead by example." Mac put a hand on his father's shoulder. "And Mom is stronger than you think."

"Stronger than me," Bobby said. And maybe it was time he changed that.

Rachel was humming when she walked into her father's house the next morning. She'd hummed that night when she went to bed, and woke up humming. While she got ready for the day, she thought about Colton's kiss. When she drove across town to her father's house, she thought about Colton's smile. And most of all, she thought about seeing Colton again tonight.

She hummed on her way into the house, the light mood lingering, even though she knew she had a huge stack of work to do, and a dying store to try to resurrect. "Good morning, Dad."

There was no answer when she entered the house. She called out again and ducked into the kitchen, expecting to find her father in his customary seat.

But he wasn't there. The song she'd been humming died in her throat. She turned down the hall, worry mushrooming in her chest, and stopped at her father's room. "Dad?"

No answer.

She turned the knob and poked her head inside. Her father was lying in his bed, the shades still drawn. "Dad?"

He cleared his throat. Roused. "Sorry, honey. Not feeling well."

She rushed over and dropped onto the side of the bed. She pressed a hand to his forehead, as if he was the child and she was the parent, but his temples were cool and dry. "What's wrong? Did you take your heart medicine yesterday?"

He thought a minute, his brow furrowed. "I don't remember."

She never should have gone out last night. Never should have left before she was sure her father was okay. "Stay right here. I'll be right back."

Rachel chided herself the whole way into the kitchen. She fixed her father some eggs, a slice of wheat toast, then poured him a glass of orange juice and grabbed his medicine. If she had stayed last night instead of going on that date, she would have made sure her father took his medication. Would have known if he had eaten before he went to bed. She saw no new dirty dishes in the sink, which meant her father had likely gone into his room to watch TV and had fallen asleep on an empty stomach.

This was all her fault. She never should have left him. Damn it.

After her father ate and took his medication, Rachel threw in some laundry and vacuumed while Ernie washed up and got dressed for the day. She tidied the kitchen, assembled a sandwich and some grapes then set the plate in the fridge for lunch. "I'll be back for dinner, Dad," she said, knowing there was no way she was going out with Colton tonight. "How about I fix Mom's meat loaf recipe?"

A soft, sad smile curved across her father's face. "That would be nice, sweetheart. Really nice."

She took off her apron and hung it on the hook inside the pantry. "Do you need anything else before I run over to the shop?"

"I've got coffee and my paper. That's all I need." He smiled at her. "I'm sorry you had to do all this. I don't mean to forget, to lose track. To—" his smile faded "—rely on you so much."

"You don't, Dad. It's fine, really."

"No, it's not." He cupped her cheek, his eyes misty. "Sometimes I just miss her so much it hurts, and I just—"

"I understand, Dad." She leaned in and pressed a kiss to his cheek. "I love you." They held gazes for a moment, then the mood lightened.

"Okay. I'll be back later." She grabbed her purse and headed for the door. Just before she put her hand on the knob, her dad spoke up.

"Did you order the new lures for fall? Folks will be coming in soon, looking for those fancy ones I showed you in the catalog."

It was the first time in a long time that her father had

given her input about the store. "Yes, I ordered them. I only got three dozen. Do you think that's enough?"

Her father thought a second. "Sounds about right. Tell Billy to increase his delivery of fresh bait. Once the kids go back to school, fishing picks up. It's not so hot out there, and all those grandpas who were stuck inside with the grandkids are itching to get out on the water."

"Sounds good, Dad." She smiled, and the urge to hum returned again. "Sounds really good."

Colton told himself he wasn't going to be overly anxious. But after spending the morning at the garage helping Luke change out a transmission, then the afternoon with Mac enjoying a leisurely lunch on the water with him and his fiancée, Savannah, Colton was feeling antsy.

He called his mom and sister back in Atlanta, but changed the subject when they asked when he was coming home. Truth be told, he wasn't sure. He'd come down to Stone Gap sure that he wouldn't stay more than a few days, just long enough to meet his brothers and father. But as one day stretched into two, three, four, the urge to leave lessened. Maybe it had something to do with Rachel.

That's why he wandered down to the hardware store a little after three that afternoon. He could see her car parked out back, and that made his steps quicken, his heart leap. He ducked into the shop, and like the first time, took a second to let his eyes adjust to the dim interior. There was one other customer at the counter, finishing up a transaction for a new tackle box. "Here you go, Mr. Allen," Rachel was saying. "Enjoy. And catch a record-breaker, will you?"

"I'm going to try," the customer said. "But I doubt anyone is ever going to break your dad's record. He's a hell of a fisherman. I sure miss seeing him around here."

"We all do," Rachel said.

The customer, a tall, thin, white-haired man, stowed the tackle box under his arm like a football. "Any idea when he'll be back behind the counter?"

"Soon." But the word had little conviction in it, and even from where he was standing, Colton could tell Rachel didn't believe her own answer.

"Well, if you see him, tell him Paul says hello. And ask him if he wants to partner up on the doubles tournament this winter. I'd sure love some of his expertise."

"I will, Mr. Allen. Thanks again."

The customer turned away and headed for the door, giving Colton a little head nod as he passed. Rachel slid the customer's check into the cash drawer then glanced over and saw Colton. A smile spread across her face, quick and bright, and that sent a little thrill through him.

There was such joy in her face when she saw him, he couldn't help but feel as though he'd hit the lottery.

"Hi," she said. "Here for another fishing pole?"

"Nope. I'm here for purely personal reasons." He closed the distance between them. He loved the way her eyes sparkled, the way her T-shirt hugged her curves. The V-neck made his gaze drop to the slight swell of her breasts. Damn, she was a beautiful woman. "I wanted to see you again. And I couldn't wait until tonight."

Her smile widened, and a faint blush crept into her cheeks. "That's very sweet. But…" She sighed. "I can't go out to dinner tonight. My dad isn't well, and he really needs me to be there, to make sure he eats and takes his medicine."

"Then bring him with us. It might do him good to get out on the town."

"Bring him with us?"

"Sure. We'll go down to the Sea Shanty. As far as I've seen, that's the most casual place this town has to offer. And the food is great. Win all around."

"You're sure you wouldn't mind having my dad along? It's not exactly a date night."

"It is if you're there." God, when did he turn into a sentimental fool? He might as well be a romance novelist, given the lines he was spouting. The worst part? It was all true. He didn't care if the entire Stone Gap High School marching band came along on their date, as long as he got to spend those hours with Rachel.

"That would be nice," she said. "But…maybe another time. I promised my dad I'd make my mother's meat loaf. It's his favorite dinner."

"Okay. I understand." Something a lot like disappointment filled his gut.

"Do you…" She paused. "Do you like meat loaf?"

"I do," Colton said. "Very much."

"Then come over. My dad would love to meet you."

He shouldn't be this excited about being invited

over for meat loaf, but he was. "Sure. Why don't I pick you up at six?"

"My car is here. I can drive myself."

"Or I can pick you up and drive you back to your car after dinner." He grinned. "In case you haven't noticed, I'm trying to grab a little alone time with you, too."

The blush deepened. "You are incorrigible."

"That's what my third grade teacher said. But I turned out okay." He leaned across the counter and placed a soft, sweet kiss on her lips. "See you at six."

And when he walked out the door a moment later, Colton Barlow was humming.

Chapter Seven

Colton was just heading into his room at the Stone Gap Inn to change his clothes when his cell phone rang. Bobby's number appeared on the caller ID, and even though Colton was far past the age where he should get excited about a call from his dad, that didn't stop his heart from doing a little skip in his chest. "Hello?"

"Hey, uh, Colton, this is... Bob—" he cleared his throat "—your dad."

Maybe Bobby was having as much trouble adjusting to the new child in his life as Colton was having adjusting to his new last name. "Yeah, hi. How are you?"

"Fine, fine."

There was a long pause while the two of them scrambled for more small talk to fill the gap in the conversation. Colton didn't know what to say. He knew so little about his father that he wasn't sure how to bridge the conversational gap. "I, uh, had breakfast with Luke and Mac the other day."

"Oh, yeah? That's good. Real good." Bobby paused again. The silence stretched, thick and uncomfortable. "Listen, every Sunday Della cooks this big dinner. Roast beef, or spaghetti, or something good. The whole family comes over. I wanted to...uh, invite you."

Wow. He'd heard about the Sunday meals from his brothers, but he hadn't been sure if Bobby would extend an invite or not. Now that he heard the words, he couldn't wait for the meal. He wondered if it would be like he'd always imagined the father and the siblings he dreamed he had in some other life. Sort of like a modern-day version of the Waltons.

Okay, so maybe he was turning into a sentimental fool. Had to be this small town. "I'd...I'd love to come. Thanks."

"Good. See you Sunday. And, uh, our anniversary party is that night. Just a small thing, over at the community center, with some local friends and you kids. Wanted to invite you to that, too. Assuming..." Bobby let out a breath.

"Assuming what?"

"Nothing, nothing. Just need to talk to Della is all." Bobby's voice sounded troubled, but Colton wasn't sure it was his place to ask his dad what was going on.

"Well, I'll see you Sunday," Colton said. "Thanks for the invites." Again, they'd exhausted their conversational abilities.

There was another uncomfortable pause, long enough

that Colton thought Bobby might have hung up. "Uh, Colton...I'm glad you're staying in town for a while," Bobby said. "And might be staying on for good. I heard Harry offered you a job."

"He did, but I haven't decided yet." Colton needed to talk to Harry first and tell him the whole story about his time in the Atlanta Fire Department. He was sure that Harry would rescind the offer after that. A fire chief wanted someone he could depend upon, and Colton wasn't so sure he was that guy.

He'd missed his job. Missed the camaraderie, the other men, his friends. But a part of him worried that maybe the worry, the doubts, he'd felt since that day would intrude when his team needed him most.

So he'd procrastinated on that conversation with Harry. A psychologist would probably say it was because Colton didn't want to face the ghosts that haunted his every thought. And maybe a little of the fact that Colton was trying to delay on the decision about staying here, investing in his family, or going back to Atlanta and leaving everything and everyone in Stone Gap behind.

"When to move on, or when to start over is a big decision to make," Bobby said. "Not something to take lightly."

It was the closest thing to advice he'd ever received from his father. The words were vague, the meaning even less clear. Was Bobby advising him to take the job or to go back to Atlanta? Maybe a little of both? "I'll keep that in mind."

"Okay, that's good. Well...I'll talk to you later."

Bobby said goodbye, and the connection went dead. Colton tucked the phone away. It wasn't quite the relationship he had come to this town to find, but it was a step in the right direction, and that was enough. For now.

A few minutes later Colton pulled in front of the hardware store just as Rachel was locking up for the night. His heart leaped at the sight of her, with her hair loose around her shoulders, her light blue T-shirt and dark-wash jeans hugging her lithe body. He hopped out of the car and pulled open the passenger-side door. A light rain began to fall, and Rachel ducked under his arm and into the car. "Thank you."

"My pleasure." He lingered a second, his arm on the door, blocking the rain from dropping onto her legs. "In case I forgot to tell you today, you look beautiful."

She laughed. "I'm wearing jeans and a T-shirt."

"And you look amazing in everything." He leaned in and kissed her. The kiss was too short, too little, but it was raining and they were late, and he would have to wait for more. "Absolutely amazing."

"You, my friend, need your vision checked."

He pulled back and gave her a grin. "Is that what we are? Friends?"

"I'm not sure what we are, Colton," she said, the playfulness dropping from her features. "And I'm not sure if I want more."

Neither was he. Hell, he didn't even know if he was staying in town. But more and more, the case for staying in Stone Gap grew stronger. For one, a new start, one far from the Atlanta FD and all the memories he had there, might be the best thing for him. Was he ever going to be able to walk into that station again and not see Willis's and Foster's faces? Would anyone he worked with ever forget? No one blamed him, but the way they talked about *the accident*, as they called it, with that little shake of their heads, made Colton feel he should have reacted faster, should have done more, should have done *something*.

But every time he looked at Rachel's smile, it made him forget for a little while. It made him wonder if maybe beginning again here, in this small town with his brothers and his father, and this intoxicating woman, might just be the solace he'd been seeking.

"I don't know either, Rachel," he said, "but I'm willing to give it some time and try to figure that out."

Then he came around to his side of the car, put the rental in gear and pulled away from the curb. The rain fell heavier now, and the wipers made steady squeaks across the windshield, trying to keep up.

"How was the shop today?" he asked. Because it was easier to change the subject than to circle around the one that didn't have any answers.

She sighed. "Slow. I'm worried I'm going to have to close. Business just hasn't been the same since my dad stopped working there. I mean, I know a lot about fishing, but I'm not him. And a lot of the old-timers came in just to chat with him. He loved that shop. Loved his job."

"And you don't love it."

She pivoted toward him. "What makes you say that?"

"I see it in your eyes. Hear it in your voice. There's nothing wrong with that, Rachel. It's not your passion, and that's okay."

"No, it's not. I told him I'd keep it running, and if I let him down, the shop will die, and then what will he have?" She let out a long breath and turned toward the window. Her breath fogged a circle against the glass. "I have to keep it running."

She sounded so dejected, he wanted to do something. But what? He sure as hell wasn't equipped to run the place for her. His heart had always been in firefighting, in the adventure of it, the puzzle of figuring out the fastest way to tame a blaze. The never knowing what the next call might hold. He was lucky enough to be doing a job that filled his soul, but he could also understand the pain of working a job that left you feeling empty at the end of the day. "Savannah was telling me that you are a wedding planner."

"I *used* to be a wedding planner. Now I'm a hammer and bait seller." She grinned, but the smile fell flat. The rain trailed in long tracks down the windows, puddling in the seals around the door. "My business has been on the back burner for a while."

"And you don't have enough time to do both."

She shook her head. "As it is, I barely have enough time for my dad. And his house…there's always twelve thousand things that need to get done. He's just been so sad since my mother died, and I just can't get him to leave the house or do anything. I wish I had the magic words to get him back to his life. Maybe then…" She sighed. "For now I'm where I need to be. If I think too much about the what-ifs, it just makes everything harder."

As if on cue, they pulled into Ernie's driveway. Colton took in the overgrown landscaping, the weedy lawn, the peeling paint on the mailbox. The rain had stopped, leaving the whole scene sparkling with fresh water drops. But that didn't make it look any less… sad, and definitely in need of some serious trimming. He could see how much work there was to do, and could only imagine how heavy that burden weighed on Rachel.

He knew what it was like to be the one everyone depended upon. He couldn't change everything for Rachel, but maybe if he started with one small thing, it would ease the weight on her shoulders. "I know my way around a lawn mower and a Weed Whacker," he said. "If you want, I can take care of the yard while you do what you need to do for your dad or the meat loaf, or whatever magic happens in the kitchen. Trust me, you'd rather have me outside than working the stove."

She blinked at him. "Really? Why would you do that?"

He looked at Rachel, at this amazing woman who was working so hard she barely had time to breathe, and his heart softened. "Because you need someone to."

Tears filled her eyes, but didn't fall. To him, that was yet another mark of how strong she was, how determined. "Thank you, Colton."

"It's no big deal." She kept looking at him as if he was this big hero, saving the day. He wasn't any of those things. He was just a guy who had offered to mow the lawn.

"It's a big deal to me. More than you know. So... thank you. In advance." She gave him a quick, tight smile, then pulled on the handle of the door and got out of the car.

Damn it. She kept looking at him like that. What would happen to that look in Rachel's eyes if he told her about Willis and Foster? He didn't want to find out, didn't want to tell her the truth. So instead of tarnishing that hero image she had in her head, he silently followed Rachel into the house to meet her father.

Rachel's father was sitting at the kitchen table, a crossword puzzle spread out before him. He had the wiry frame of someone who had been active all his life, and short gray hair that smoothed across his head. His glasses perched on the end of his nose, secured to his neck by a dark brown chain. He took them off and let them dangle against his chest when Colton and Rachel came into the kitchen. "You brought company," he said to Rachel.

"I brought someone who actually volunteered to tackle that weedy mess you call a yard, Dad." Rachel leaned in and pressed a kiss to her father's cheek. "Dad, this is Colton Barlow. Colton, this is my father, Ernie."

"The fishing champion," Colton said, extending his hand. "I've heard quite a lot about you from Harry Washington."

Ernie got to his feet and shook hands with Colton. His skin was pale, his grip a little weak, as if he'd spent a lot of time at this kitchen table. Given the state of the yard and the fact that Rachel was running the shop alone, Colton was pretty positive the only place Ernie had visited lately was this one room. "Harry? How is that old bastard?"

"Fine, sir. Just fine."

Ernie slid an amused glance in Rachel's direction. "So this is the one you bought the dress and fancy shoes for?"

Rachel blushed. "Dad!"

Colton grinned. "You bought a new dress for our date?"

"I *needed* a new dress. That was the only reason why."

"Don't let her fool you," Ernie said, leaning in toward Colton. "She was as nervous as a chicken in a doghouse. So, Colton…Barlow? I know the Barlows. How are you related to Bobby?"

Small-town living—obviously everyone who heard Colton's last name was going to ask that same question. "Uh, he's my father. I'm Luke, Jack and Mac's half brother."

"Oh, okay. Well, welcome to Stone Gap." Ernie sat back down at the table and picked up his crossword puzzle. He sat his glasses on his nose again. Apparently, that was all he needed to know.

"Dad, Colton was going to go work on the yard. I'm going to make the meat loaf. Maybe you want to help Colton?"

Her father scowled. "I have the crossword to do."

Rachel started to say something, then instead let

out a long sigh that said she'd been down this road a dozen times. "Okay."

Colton could see the frustration in her eyes. He knew that feeling. There'd been times with his mother when she would sink into a deep depression, and it would be like pulling rope through a needle to get her motivated again. He'd done what he could to take over the care of his little sister, and to cover for their mother, who had often put her children second. He didn't think Rachel's father was like that, but he could certainly relate to the challenges she faced. "Mr. Morris, I don't need your help, but I sure would appreciate you showing me where all the yard tools are."

Ernie dropped his glasses to his chest again. "'Spose I can do that." He got to his feet, tugged a key off the hook by the back door then beckoned to Colton to follow him.

As Colton passed Rachel, she gave him a grateful smile and mouthed, "thank you." For that smile, Colton decided, he would do about anything.

Rachel watched through the window as Colton and her father headed into the shed. She held her breath, sure that in a few minutes, her father would be back in the kitchen, sitting in the same chair, holding the same pen, working on the same crossword puzzle.

But then she saw her father emerge from the shed with the hedge trimmers in one hand. He was talking to Colton as he walked across the yard and gesturing toward the edge of the lawn. Colton nodded then turned back to the lawn mower. A moment later the mower was roaring along the grass, cutting it to a fraction of its overgrown length. Her father was wielding the gas hedge trimmers like a ninja with a sword, taming the wild shrubbery into something resembling its former self.

She smiled and started humming again as she chopped vegetables then mixed up the meat loaf and got it into the oven. While her father and Colton worked on the yard, she whipped up some mashed potatoes and baked a batch of brownies from a mix she found in the cupboard. By the time the men came in, a little sweaty, a little dirty and a lot hungry, dinner was ready and on the table.

"I'm about tuckered out now," Ernie said, swiping at the sweat on his brow. "I think that's the most work I've done in a year."

"The yard should be good for a while now," Colton said. "I'll come by next week and give it another mow."

Next week? Did that mean Colton was thinking of staying?

Rachel handed each of them a glass of ice water. "You guys did a great job. The yard looks amazing."

Ernie put a hand on his daughter's back. "That's a good man you found. I'd keep him around if I were you. I'm going to go wash up for supper. Be right back."

She couldn't have been more shocked at the change in her father if she tried. He had a little color in his cheeks, a little spring in his step. And all because of whatever Colton had said to him that got her father outside and working.

Once her father was out of earshot, Colton turned to Rachel. "Seems I got the paternal vote of approval."

She grinned. "That doesn't mean you move out of the friend category."

Colton leaned in close to her, so close she could feel the heat of his skin, catch the whisper of his cologne. She watched his pulse tick in his neck. "What's a man got to do to impress you, Rachel Morris?"

She swallowed hard and thought it was a good thing they weren't alone in the house. She wanted this man, with his lopsided smile and his easy way with her father, in the worst possible way. In the kind of way that clouded all rational thought and pushed all her pretty little reasons for not having a relationship off a mental cliff. "I think you're already doing it, Colton Barlow."

Colton grinned then pulled away and turned to wash his hands in the sink. "Good to know. Maybe I should do more of whatever it is I'm doing right."

"What did you say to my dad that got him to work with you?"

"My mom would go through these periods of depression." Colton picked up a dish towel, leaned against the counter and dried his hands over and over again. "There were days when neither me nor my sister could get her to eat, never mind get out of bed. A thousand times, I was patient, and took care of Katie, and helped her. But then one day I went in there and asked her if this was how she wanted her kids to remember her, because she was killing herself, one day at a time."

"You said that to my father?"

"Not in that way. I was a little nicer in how I said

it to your dad. I mentioned that he had a really great daughter who wanted to spend some quality time with him. Your dad cursed a couple times then grabbed the hedge trimmers and said he better do them himself because I wouldn't know the way he liked the shrubs to look. But he wasn't mad at me. More…concerned about you."

She laughed. "That sounds like my dad."

"He took it well. And by the time the lawn was finished, we were buddies. With my mom, she got out of bed and never really sank to that same level of depression."

"Thank you." The two words were as thick as paste in her throat. They couldn't come close to expressing her gratitude, how deep that thanks reached inside her. With a simple household chore, Colton had fostered the change that Rachel had been trying to create for over a year.

"It was nothing."

"No, Colton, it was everything." She swiped at her eyes, cursing the tears that sprang there. Colton chuckled softly and stepped forward with the dish towel.

"Don't cry, Rachel. It was only yard work." He dabbed at the tears on her face and then cupped her cheek. "Okay?"

She nodded, and the tears gave way to laughter. "Maybe so, but it was a *lot* of yard work."

"Which means I'm hoping there's a *lot* of dinner as a reward."

She would have made a month's worth of meals

to thank him if she could have. "Oh, there is, Colton, there definitely is."

Her father came into the kitchen. "Watch out, you two lovebirds. Old man coming in the room."

"Dad, we're not—"

"Definitely not," Colton added.

Ernie chuckled. "Whatever you two say. Now, let's eat."

Her father was laughing. Of all the things that had happened in the last couple hours, hearing the sound of her father's laughter filled Rachel's heart with joy. For the first time in a really long time, she had hope. It was still fragile, but it was there. She could see a new road ahead—if her father kept going in the right direction.

Her father sat at the head of the table, with Colton and Rachel on either side of him. He glanced around the dining room, and his eyes grew misty. "We haven't had a meal in this room in a long, long time."

"Too long, I think," she said. It was something she needed to change. Maybe now that her father was coming back to his life, he would step outside that kitchen, in more ways than one.

"Your mom used to do such great Sunday dinners, didn't she? Before she got…sick."

That was the term they all used to describe her mother's alcoholism. The years before she got sick. Maybe that made it easier, Rachel thought, to accept her mother's choices. But it didn't ease her guilty feelings about not being here at the end, not getting that closure and, most of all, leaving her father to deal with it all.

"I thought it would be more comfortable to eat in the dining room," she said. "And maybe a way to kind of include Mom, too."

Ernie's eyes watered. "She'd like that."

Rachel covered her dad's hand with her own. His weathered palm grasped hers, tight and sure. "Thanks, Dad."

Ernie's smile wobbled on his face, then he cleared his throat, dismissing the moment, moving on. Her father wasn't a man given to expressing his emotions much, and it didn't surprise her when he grabbed the bowl of mashed potatoes and started dishing them up. "Let's eat before this all gets cold."

They shared the dishes around, family style, and the conversation gradually turned from the condition of the lawn to the weather to Colton. "So, what do you do for work?" Ernie asked.

"I'm a firefighter, sir. With the Atlanta Fire Department."

"But Harry offered him a job here," Rachel added. A big part of her hoped Colton took the job. She definitely wanted to spend more time with this man who had made her father laugh and brought some sun to his cheeks.

Not to mention that every time she was within a few feet of him, she couldn't help but gravitate closer to Colton. Even sitting at the table with him, Rachel had this awareness of Colton, a constant hum in her body.

Ernie forked up some more meat loaf, already on his second helping. "Harry's a good man. He runs that department like a tight ship, but he's fair and smart. I've known him most all my life."

"I'm thinking about his job offer," Colton said. He toyed with his food. "I haven't decided anything yet."

But he had decided to stay another week, which she took as a good sign.

"Atlanta must be a busy department," Rachel said. "I've only been to the city a few times, but it seemed like it was always hopping."

"It was." Colton shifted in his seat.

"Firefighting's a pretty noble profession," her father said. "My cousin was a firefighter. He lost a leg in a blaze. Got caught under some falling timbers. But the other guys were right there, thank God, and pulled him out. He still gets together with those guys once a week, even though he had to leave the department."

"That would be tough," Colton said. "Can you, uh, pass the potatoes?"

Rachel did as he asked then cut off a bite of meat loaf. "So, what was the biggest fire you ever had to fight?"

Colton's entire demeanor shifted into stone. He dropped the mashed potatoes back into the serving bowl and pushed it to the side. "I, uh, don't really want to talk about my job over dinner and bore you all. I'd much rather hear about Ernie's fishing tips. Since I don't know much about fishing, and if I'm going to keep up with Rachel here, then I should learn some insider secrets."

That got her dad talking for the next twenty minutes about lures and rods and secret fishing holes. The two men conversed like old friends, and by the time the dinner dishes were cleared and the dishwasher was loaded, Rachel could see her father flagging. It had been a lot of activity for one day, after almost a year of nothing.

Ernie stood in the kitchen beside his daughter, sipping a glass of water after taking his heart medication. "This was a good night. A good meal."

"It was, Dad." She leaned into him and gave him a hug. "It was good to see you feeling better."

"Yeah." He started to say something else when a pair of headlights appeared in the driveway. "Huh. Who's here at this time of night?"

Rachel knew, because most nights she was still up, doing the dishes or working on paperwork, and making sure her dad didn't need anything. Ernie Morris was normally in bed before eight at night, claiming he was tired as soon as the evening meal was done. But tonight, between the yard work and the conversation with Colton, eight had stretched into eight thirty, and that meant Daryl was coming by for his usual weekly check-in on her dad.

Rachel got to her feet and opened the door. "Great timing," she said to Daryl. "I made brownies."

"Who are you offering my brownies to?" her father called from behind her. "And why haven't I heard about them until now?"

"I was saving them in case we had company." Rachel opened the door the rest of the way and stepped back. Her father had made great strides this evening. She could only hope the change would continue, courtesy of a little brownie bribery.

Daryl strode in, ducking his head a little under the jamb. He was a tall, lanky man, whose clothes never quite matched the length of his arms and legs. He wore a floppy fisherman's hat everywhere he went, no matter the time of day. He'd grown a beard this year, and the reddish-brown hair on his face made him look a little like a skinny lumberjack. "Ernie. How you doing?" he said, as if no more than an afternoon had passed since he'd last seen his friend.

Rachel tensed. Her father had made it clear over the last year that he didn't want company. Didn't want his friends paying "sympathy visits."

Her father looked at Daryl, then at Rachel, then back at Daryl again. "Well, don't just stand in the doorway. Come on in. Rachel says there's brownies, and we might as well eat them."

"Good thinking on the brownies," Colton whispered to Rachel.

Daryl took a seat at the kitchen table beside Ernie. "It's about damned time you invited me in. You are a pain in the ass, you know that?"

Daryl was probably the only human being in the world that could say that to her father. Ernie grinned. "Hey, we all got to be good at something."

Rachel dished up the brownies and brewed a pot of decaf while her father introduced Colton, and the three of them talked about fishing. It was an ordinary scene, something that could be happening in a million houses across the world at this very moment. And that was what made it perfect. Absolutely, wonderfully perfect.

Chapter Eight

It wasn't just the meat loaf and brownies that had Colton falling for Rachel. It was the way she took care of her father, the way she worried and tended, but didn't hover. She was a woman with a generous heart, and that drew him to her in ways he'd never been drawn to a woman before.

It was that way she had about her that had him thinking about something that lasted a lot longer than tonight. Something that involved dinners around a table and teasing while they stood at the sink, finishing up the dishes.

He reached across the console while he drove her home and took her hand in his. It felt nice. Perfect. Right.

When she'd mentioned she was tired, he offered to

bring her home, instead of back to her car at the shop, because that would also give him an excuse to pick her up again in the morning. He didn't have anything planned for tomorrow, so maybe he could take Rachel to breakfast, drop her off at work then swing by Ernie's again and tackle the leaky sink in the hall bathroom, or do some touch-up painting on the front of the house.

Rachel turned and smiled at him. "Thank you. Again. I haven't seen my father that interested in life in a long, long time. I can't believe he was still talking to Daryl when we left."

"Making plans for fishing trips, too."

"*And* he said he was going to come to the shop tomorrow." Her smile widened. "If my dad gets back to work, then maybe…maybe eventually I can get back to my business."

"Planning all those happily-ever-afters for everyone?"

She laughed. "Exactly."

"And what about you?" He took a right onto Main Street and drove past the dark, closed stores that lined the downtown area.

"What about me?"

"Why hasn't some very smart man married you yet?" Had he just asked that question? It had to be the sugar overload from the brownies. Colton wasn't looking to settle down. Especially not in this little town. But then he thought of the dinner, the laughter, the smile on Rachel's face, the feel of her beside him in the kitchen, in the car. And thought if this was settling down, it wouldn't be so bad. Not at all.

"Maybe I've just been an even smarter woman who hasn't wanted to marry any of those men," she said.

He chuckled. "Touché."

"And what about you? Why haven't you gotten married yet?"

"To be honest, I haven't met anyone who made me want to stay in one place long enough to put a ring on it." Until now. Until this woman with her determination and her caring came along and made him want something more. A lot more.

"This isn't exactly second date conversation," she said with a slight laugh in her voice. "Aren't we still supposed to be talking about our favorite pets or what we were like in fourth grade?"

"My favorite pet was my dog Tommy, a little mixed breed spaniel. I got him when I was six, and he lived until my senior year of high school. Someday, I'll get another dog, but working as a firefighter..." He shrugged. "I can't leave a dog overnight several days a week. And as for fourth grade, let's just say my report card had big words on it like overly enthusiastic and stubbornly energetic."

Rachel laughed. "Stubbornly energetic?"

"My fourth grade teacher was trying to nicely say I was a complete pain in the neck." He grinned.

"Now that, I believe." She sat back against the seat. The golden glow from the streetlights danced highlights in her hair as they drove, and speckled diamonds across her skin. "My favorite pet was a turtle I kept in a tank in my room. I always wanted a dog, but my mom was allergic. So I had a turtle, until I went to college. Then I gave him to my little cousin Sharlene, who promised to take good care of him."

"And did she?"

"He's still alive, last I heard. Sharlene became a veterinary tech, so I think my turtle is in safe hands. And I'd like to think I was part of what drove her into animal care."

"Look at that. A turtle inspiring a life of giving back to the animal kingdom."

"Exactly. As for fourth grade, I was the one getting all As and receiving the perfect-attendance award."

"Teacher's pet?" He pulled to a stop in the parking lot of her apartment building and turned the car off.

"Not exactly. I guess…" She shrugged. "My childhood was kind of chaotic and I guess I thought if I kept everything perfect at school, maybe that would make things better at home. Crazy thinking."

"Not when you're in fourth grade." He unbuckled, then reached across to brush a long blond lock off her forehead. "I know how hard it is to be the one who feels responsible."

And to be the one who had let others down. Who had tried his best, and his best still hadn't been enough. To be the one left behind, with guilt and regret sitting on either shoulder.

She cupped his jaw and met his gaze with her own. "You made everything different today and I…I really appreciate it."

God, she was beautiful. He was drawn to her intensity, the way her gaze seemed to hold him captive. He couldn't have left right now if he tried. "Really, it was nothing. I'm just glad I was there. But you know what I'm even more grateful for?"

Her eyes widened, and a tease lit her face. "What?"

"Meeting you." He leaned closer, fumbling with one hand for the button at her waist. He released the seat belt, and it retracted with a soft whoosh. Colton closed the distance between them and kissed Rachel.

He'd intended a simple, easy good-night kiss. One that would punctuate the thank-yous with one of his own. *Thank you for including me. Thank you for looking at me like I'm someone amazing. Thank you for making my days brighter.*

But she let out a little moan as he kissed her, and all those simple, easy intentions disappeared. He groaned, and the kiss deepened. His hands roamed over her hair, her shoulders, her back, and her touch matched his, sliding down the back of his arms, around to his waist, back again.

The stupid console sat between them like a wall. The bucket seats felt too small, too confined. He briefly considered climbing over the console, but was pretty sure he'd risk serious injury with the gear shift.

"Let's go inside," she whispered against his mouth.

Thank God. "I think that's the best idea I've heard all day." They broke apart just long enough to get out of the car then meet up again on the walkway. His arm went around her waist; his head dipped to kiss her again, the heat building as they walked and kissed, and tried to hurry without running into a wall.

An interminable minute later, they were on the third floor of her building and she was cursing as she tried to jam the key into the lock. Colton closed his hand over hers and the key slid into place, then turned and the lock released. They stumbled into her apartment, and he kicked the door shut then kiss-walked down the hall to her bedroom. Rachel nudged the bedroom door open with her hip. Colton scooped her up, thinking how light and perfect she felt in his arms, then he took a few steps forward and laid her on the bed.

"You look incredible," he said. Even that wasn't the right word for how beautiful she was, in the darkened room, with only the moonlight dancing through the windows, casting her in an ethereal glow.

"And you look...tempting." A slow, seductive smile curved across her face as she rose up on her elbows then reached out and tugged him forward by a belt loop. "Too tempting."

"I could say the same about you." He reached for the hem of her T-shirt and tugged it up and over her head, revealing a lacy white bra beneath. He ran a finger along the scalloped edge then dipped inside the cup and brushed against her nipple. She gasped, and that made him smile. "Very, very tempting."

That blush he loved filled her cheeks. "I wore it because... Well, I didn't know..."

Just the thought that she had worn this for him, on the off chance they'd end up here, flattered Colton. He would have to show her how very much.

He reached for the fly of her jeans. She lifted her hips and he undid the fastener, then the zipper, and tugged the denim off. When he saw the scrap of matching panties, he dropped the jeans on the floor, not even caring where they ended up.

He climbed onto the bed, and Rachel lay down beneath him, her eyes wide, her mouth slightly open, anticipation filling her face. He brushed a kiss across her lips, her cheeks, then down her jaw, along her neck, lingering in the valley of her shoulders. She arched against him, and he splayed his palm, sliding it down her belly, over the mound between her legs, feeling her through the lace. She was wet already, ready for him, but he wasn't about to rush something this incredible.

He kissed every inch of skin between her neck and her breasts. She was warm and sweet, and smelled like vanilla and spice. He peeled down the silky strap of her bra, one side then the other, and her breasts rose above the lacy cups. He nudged back the lace and took one nipple in his mouth. Rachel gasped, and when he put his hand between her legs, she ground against the touch. Her breathing came in faster and faster gasps. Then he slid a finger under the lace of her panties and rubbed at the tender, hard bud between her legs, never taking his attention off her nipple. Rachel bucked up against him and let out a long, long, shuddering breath.

"Oh…oh, my. That…that's never happened before. Not…that easily." Another of those blushes he loved appeared on her cheeks.

"Then we should do it again. And again." He grinned.

"First, I think we should be equally naked." She tugged at his shirt, working her way through the buttons then sliding it over and off his shoulders. Her hands followed the fabric's path down his arms until it lay on the floor and her hands had slid around to his waist. She undid the button fly and shoved his jeans and underwear down in one fell swoop.

He climbed onto the bed beside her and rolled Rachel on top of him, undoing the clasp on the back of her bra, then urging her panties down and off. He reached over the side of the bed, tugged his wallet out of his back pocket and found a condom.

"Let me," she whispered, taking the foil packet from him. She nudged him onto his back then straddled his thighs, and in one deft movement, unfurled the condom and slid it along his erection.

This woman was full of surprises. He'd expected someone who blushed as easily as she did to be shy in bed, but as Rachel raised her hips and slid onto his sheathed penis, he realized she was anything but shy. And he was pretty much done thinking for a while.

She was glorious on top of him, riding him with sure and steady strokes, her breasts full and perfect in the moonlight. He cupped them with his palms, letting his thumbs circle over the nipples. She clutched his hands and moaned, then increased her pace.

She arched back a little, deepening his entry into her, and a second later she was riding him hard and fast, and the gasps were turning into breathless words of nothing, and then she came again, and he damned near lost it.

Instead, he flipped her over and braced himself above her head. "You are amazing. Surprising. Intoxicating."

That blush again, that captivating blush that had

him hooked from the first day. "And you are a serious flatterer."

"Because I'm—" He let out a breath, figured why not say it; where had not saying how he felt gotten him in life? "Falling for you."

"Falling...for me?"

"Falling," he whispered, dancing a finger across her lips, "for you. In a big way."

She smiled, and that sweet smile hit him somewhere deep in his chest. Suddenly, this wasn't sex, it wasn't a moment of relief, it was more. A connection.

And when he slid into her, she reached up to draw him even closer and their strokes quickened, the connection quadrupled, and Colton knew he wasn't just falling for Rachel Morris—he was falling hard.

Chapter Nine

Colton left a little after midnight. As content as Rachel had felt, curled in his arms after some seriously amazing sex, a level of panic began to set in when her mind finally processed the words *I'm falling for you.*

Because she was falling for him, too, and that thought scared the hell out of her. He wasn't staying in town—as far as she knew—and she still had a life too full for a relationship. The old familiar fears, the same ones that had made her keep all her other boyfriends at arm's length, began to creep in. What if she fell for him and made a mistake? Landed in an unhappy marriage, like her parents had?

She'd planned dozens of weddings, watched dozens of couples say I do. And at the end of the year, maybe six out of ten were still as happy as the day they walked down the aisle. She'd seen the giddy, infatuated stage yield to frustration and resentment, and watched those very dreams dissolve for some of the couples she had worked for. It had made her skittish, unwilling to risk her own heart.

Until she met Colton.

And now, in the warm glow of the dark hours after he had left, lying in her bed, with the scent of him still on her sheets and skin, she began to wonder if maybe… just maybe, it was time for her fairy tale, too.

Colton wound his way through the dark streets of Stone Gap, with Rachel's building growing more and more distant in his rearview mirror. He should have stayed in her bed, with her in his arms, but after saying he was falling for her, he'd begun to realize how quickly this had all become so cozy and intimate, and that maybe it would be a good idea to apply the brakes.

Okay, so he was a guy and he thought of that *after* they'd made love.

He'd realized how easy it would be to fall asleep in that bed, to spend a night with her and wake up to her smile—and all the implications that would come with that. Like that he was staying around. That he wanted something permanent here in Stone Gap. When he wasn't sure what he wanted or where he was going.

A storm was beginning to brew, and lightning crackled in the sky, some bolts so close it bathed the car's interior in white, but Colton hardly noticed. His mind was back on Rachel. He missed her already, and had started missing her the second he said goodbye.

Half of him wanted to turn around. The other half said it was a good thing he hadn't stayed.

This town was settling on him, like easing into a comfortable sweater. Tomorrow morning, he decided, he was going to go to Harry Washington and tell him about what had happened in Atlanta. And if Harry still wanted him to be part of the Stone Gap Fire Department, then Colton was going to take the job. Atlanta no longer held the appeal that this tiny town—and one particular woman in this town—did.

As he turned the corner onto Main Street, he saw a flicker of light ahead of him. At first he thought it was a streetlight going bad, but then the flicker showed orange, and he knew, with that pit of dread in his stomach, what the light really meant.

Fire.

He had no gear, he had no hose, no water. He gunned the car and closed the distance between himself and the flickering flames. The fire was licking up the side of the building housing Ernie's Hardware. Colton brought the car to a stop, dug out his phone and dialed 9-1-1.

"There's a fire at the intersection of Main and Berry," he said to the dispatcher. "Small, but not contained, on the exterior wall of the hardware shop."

"Is anyone inside?" the dispatcher asked.

"Not that—" Then Colton saw a shadow pass in front of the window and he let out a curse. "Yes, yes, someone's inside. I'm going in."

"Sir, wait for the fire department. Sir—"

But Colton was already gone, and the dispatcher was talking to the empty interior of his car.

The flames were moving faster now, spreading up the wooden exterior so quickly it seemed the fire was devouring the building like a late-night snack. In minutes it would be inside, and whoever was inside the building—

Colton didn't finish that train of thought. He ran across the street, straight toward the wood-and-glass door of the shop. He tried the handle, but it was locked. He pounded on the door, but there was no response. Had he really seen someone? Or was it his imagination?

He peered into the glass, but the interior was dark. Nothing but shapes, straight edges of shelves and boxes. Then the flames ate through the exterior wall, and orange light danced over the shop. Maybe he'd been mistaken. Maybe he'd seen the reflection of a passing car or something else.

There, on the floor, was the shape of a man. Oh, God. He wasn't moving.

Colton drew back and slammed his shoulder against the door. It refused to yield. He did it again. A third time. The door was thick and locked tight.

Panic drummed in his chest, but he tamped it down. Focus—that was what he needed to do. Focus on what he had been trained to do.

He spun around, looking for something, anything to help him gain entry. The sound of sirens began to rise in the distance, but they were too far away. They'd never make it in time. If he didn't get in there—

No. He wasn't going to think about that. This wasn't Willis and Foster. And there was still time for Colton to find a way in, to save whoever was lying on that floor.

He saw a small wooden bench outside the shop next door. He yanked it up and hurled it through the plate-glass window, straight through the display of tackle boxes and waders and the small sign advertising night crawlers. The closed sign blinked and then went out, as the glass shattered and the window fell apart in a cacophony of sound.

Colton climbed over the sill, careful not to touch the jagged edges. "Where are you?" he called out.

No response.

"I'm coming to get you. Just hold on." He didn't know if he was talking to someone who was still alive, but that didn't stop Colton from moving forward.

The flames were growing on the eastern wall, shivering up the paneled interior like macabre curtains. The smoke was growing thicker, and Colton raised his arm to cover his mouth. His eyes watered, his throat burned and the heat was rising, threatening to burn. But he pushed forward, shoving aside the jumbled mess from the broken window. He rounded the corner, passing the very register where he had first seen Rachel, and there, on the floor, was Ernie.

He wasn't moving. In the dark, Colton wasn't even sure if he was breathing. There was no time to check. There was only hoisting Ernie onto his shoulders and turning for the exit as the flames caught the new inrush of air and spread into the room like a mushroom cloud.

* * *

The phone was ringing.

Rachel clawed her way out of a deep sleep, vaguely aware that this wasn't a dream, and fumbled for her phone on the bedside table. "Hello?"

"Rachel? It's Harry Washington."

The fire chief? Why was he calling her at—she glanced at the clock—two thirty in the morning? After Colton had left, she had spent an hour or so working on a plan that might—just might—allow her to take on Ginny's wedding and work at the shop, before finally going to sleep a little after one. She struggled into a sitting position and pushed the hair out of her eyes. "Okay."

"There's been a fire at the store. Your dad was there, but—"

Fire? Her father? Had she heard Harry right? No, it was impossible. Her father was sitting at the kitchen table talking to Daryl when she left. "Are you sure? Is he okay? Where is he?"

"He's at the hospital," Harry said. "He's…he's had a tough time of it, and I don't know what his condition is right now. But Colton is there with him."

"I'm on my way." She hung up the phone, pulled on the first clothes she could find and ran out the door. She drove through town, taking the turn that would take her past the store.

All this time, she'd been hoping Harry was wrong. That it was some kind of terrible prank call. But the sight of the Stone Gap Fire Department fire trucks parked on Main Street, the firefighters hosing down the last of the embers and the acrid, heavy scent of burned wood and plastic spoke the truth. *Oh, God. Dad.*

Rachel detoured from the chaos in front of the store and concentrated on getting to the hospital. Whatever had happened to the shop—and whether it was salvageable or not—would have to wait. It didn't matter, as long as her father was okay.

A few minutes later she'd arrived at the small local hospital and found her father's room. The hospital was quiet, save for the occasional beep of a machine and the low murmur of voices in other rooms. She ducked into his room, her heart in her throat.

Colton sat in the chair beside her father's bed. He had his head in his hands, his pale blue shirt smudged with soot, his hair and face mussed and dirty. He looked up when she entered and got to his feet.

"How is he?" she whispered. She almost didn't want to ask the question. Didn't want to hear that her father had some fatal injury or that he wasn't going to wake up. She could see his still body beneath the white sheets, looking thin and fragile.

"He's exhausted. Suffered some smoke inhalation, but he's going to be okay." Colton moved in front of her and waited until her gaze met his. "He's going to be fine, Rachel. Just fine."

She peered around Colton. To her, her father looked far from fine. "Are you sure?"

Colton cupped her cheeks and waited for her to look at him again. "Yes, I'm sure."

Only then did relief flood the places that had been

filled with panic. Only then could she focus on Colton for a second, on his sooty clothes and the way he smelled like smoke. "What happened to you? Why are you such a mess?"

"Because that damned fool jumped through the window to save this damned fool," her father muttered from the bed.

Rachel dashed to her father's bedside and sank onto the mattress. She took her father's hand in her own. "Dad. Are you okay?"

Her father's eyes fluttered open and he nodded. He coughed, then cleared his throat, but still his voice remained raspy. "Nothing a little time at home can't solve. Once they let me out of this place. Doctor wants me to stay overnight."

She pressed her cheek to her father's, so happy to have the rough stubble of his unshaven face against hers, to smell the Old Spice cologne he'd worn as long as she could remember. His cologne was mixed with the smell of smoke, but he was here, alive and complaining and exactly the way he'd always been. "What were you doing in the store late at night?"

"Got it in my foolish head that I wanted to check on things. I got all excited by today and talking to Daryl about fishing. Made me miss the place. I couldn't sleep—" he paused to cough "—so I walked down there and thought I'd just see how the old girl was holding up. Lightning hit the building and next thing I know, it's hotter than hell and I can't breathe. They say I passed out, but I don't remember much after the lightning."

She hugged him tight. Later, she would lecture him about going to the shop alone, in the middle of the night, especially with a storm in the air. But for now she had gratitude, and she didn't want to spoil that moment of blessing. "I'm so glad you're okay."

"Thank Colton," her father said. "I can't believe he did such a stupid thing."

"It wasn't stupid, sir. It was my job."

She turned to Colton and reached for his hand, drawing him into the circle of light cast by the lamp over her father's head. How did she get so lucky to have this man drop into her life at exactly the right time? She wanted to thank him, but her heart filled her throat.

"You're welcome," Colton said softly, then his gaze cut away.

Every time she thanked him or praised him, he brushed it off. Because he was humble? Embarrassed? She didn't care. He deserved the praise times a thousand. She squeezed his fingers. "See? I told you that you're a hero."

"No, I'm not, Rachel." His eyes clouded over and his body tensed. "Please stop saying that. I got lucky this time. It might not happen again." He walked to the door, then turned back to meet her confused, hurt gaze. "I'm glad your father is okay."

Then he turned on his heel and left the room. The scent of smoke still lingered in the air, but the danger had already passed.

Chapter Ten

Colton paced his room at the Stone Gap Inn then took a walk and finally returned to his room to pace again for the rest of the night—in the few hours of darkness left—feeling useless. Yes, he'd gotten Ernie out in time, but he hadn't been there soon enough to stop the fire, to stop Ernie from even entering the building in the first place. He should have seen it sooner, should have reacted faster. Maybe then Rachel's father wouldn't be lying in a hospital bed.

He wanted to do *something* but he didn't know what. He couldn't rewind time, couldn't correct yet another time when he had been too late—too damned late.

Damn.

He paced, he thought, he cursed. Then, shortly after dawn broke across Stone Gap and the sun began to fill his room with light, Colton had a plan. He had his phone out and was dialing before he realized how early it was.

Luke's groggy voice came across the phone line. "If you weren't my brother, I would have to kill you for waking me up this early."

Colton chuckled. "I'm sorry. I forgot what time it was."

"Then call me back when the little hand gets past the eight. You know which one is the little hand, right?"

"Don't hang up, Luke. This can't wait."

Luke sighed. There was rustling in the background while Luke got out of bed and let out another tired sigh. "Okay, shoot."

Colton explained about the fire, about what had happened to Ernie, then laid out his plan to his brother. After several days of seeing Luke and Mac, it was easier to think of them as his brothers. As part of his family. "I know Jack is due back from his honeymoon tomorrow morning, so I don't know if we can count on him. And I don't want to wait another day if I can help it."

"He's a Barlow. Of course you can count on him," Luke said. "You can count on all of us."

That sounded good to Colton's ears. Really good. "Thanks, Luke. I appreciate it."

"Did you tell Dad? Back in the day, he was pretty handy. Taught us everything we know." There was the sound of running water then the *glug-glug* of a coffeepot starting up. "And I know he and Ernie go way back."

"I wasn't sure if I should call him or not." Truth be told, Colton was feeling like a teenager who didn't want to be rejected. Yes, his father had invited him to Sunday dinner, but he hadn't talked to Colton otherwise. Colton kept holding off on reaching out. Okay, yeah, he was being a coward.

"You can't know if he'll say yes unless you do," Luke said. "But a word to the wise…"

"Yeah?"

"Wait till after seven." Luke chuckled. "I'll see you down there in about an hour. Okay?"

Colton hung up with Luke then got busy making a list of supplies. He left the inn, walked downtown to grab a cup of coffee at the Good Eatin' Café then drummed his fingers on the table, waiting for the clock to tick past seven. Once it did, Colton dialed his father's number, but got the voice mail. He left a quick, short message then hung up.

"Can I give you a refill?" Viv, the gregarious owner of the Good Eatin' Café, said as she approached his table with a fresh pot of coffee.

"Yes, ma'am. Thank you. That would be great."

"Brownie points for you, young man. You called me *ma'am*." She smiled and patted his shoulder. "I saw you and Rachel Morris here the other night. She's mighty lucky to have you. You two make a wonderful couple."

Colton wasn't so sure Rachel had him, nor was he sure she wanted him to be in her life after last night. Yes, she was grateful he had rescued her dad, but he should have been there sooner, gotten into the building faster. Then maybe Ernie wouldn't be lying in a hospital bed. And once he told Rachel what had happened to Willis and Foster…

That shining light in her eyes that saw him as a hero would definitely dim.

Viv let out a sigh as her gaze went out the window to the smoky, charred remains across the street. "Terrible thing what happened to Ernie's store. That man has been through enough. What with his wife being so needy all those years, then her dying and then poor Rachel trying to fill his shoes. Now this? Goodness, that family has had enough heartbreak to last a lifetime."

"I agree," Colton said. "Ernie's a real nice man. I got to know him pretty well this week."

"He's part of the same quality stock as most folks in this town. You're included in that." Viv pointed a finger at him. "You're a Barlow, through and through."

"Half Barlow."

"The better half," she said with a smile. "And you know, you may have come about being a Barlow in a little bit different way from Luke, Mac and Jack, but folks 'round here, they'll see you as the same. Just give 'em time."

"I'm not worried about what people think about me. I am what I am, and if they don't like it…" He shrugged.

"That is a good attitude to have." She patted his shoulder again. "Harry was right. You're gonna fit in just fine in Stone Gap."

He shouldn't be surprised that the owner of the diner knew just about as much about him as he knew about himself. It was, after all, a very small town, and word spread faster than chicken pox here. "I haven't decided if I'm staying yet."

She glanced at the paper on the table before him, the list he'd bulleted while he was waiting. A smile crossed her face. "Oh, you have already. You just don't know it."

The owner of the café walked away, just as Luke and Mac came in through the door and sat across from him. Viv came back with coffees for both of them and promised hearty breakfasts in a jiffy.

"I think we've got about everything on your list," Luke said. "The rest should be delivered at a *reasonable* hour of the morning."

Mac laughed. "You still complaining about having to wake up before noon? You know, you're about to be a married man, Luke. With a kid, at that. Those bachelor days of sleeping off a hangover are over."

"For your information, I was up late reading to a five-year-old who got scared by the storm." Luke gave Mac a *so-there* glare. "I have reformed my ways and have become a card-carrying family man."

"There is hope for humanity." Mac grinned then let out an *oomph* when Luke slugged him.

"So, did you call Dad?" Luke asked.

"Left him a voice mail." Colton shrugged. "I don't know if he'll show up."

"He'll show." Luke nodded. "Have faith."

That was the one thing Colton had lost a while ago. Faith. Especially in himself. In his future. Every time he thought he might be finding his way again, something like last night happened. A too-close call that reminded him of what he had lost.

The three of them ate breakfast, with Colton getting an extra order of bacon and toast after all, then paid the bill, leaving a generous tip for Viv, and headed across the street. The acrid smell of burned wood still hung in the air, and steam rose from what remained of the still-warm eastern wall of the shop. Half of it had crumbled in the fire, leaving the inside of the store exposed to the elements.

"Okay," Luke said, "let's get this party started." He reached in the back of his truck, pulling out sledgehammers, shovels and crowbars for the three of them. They set to work, dismantling the burned half of the building and stacking the debris to the side. By nine o'clock, the Dumpster had arrived, along with a delivery of fresh lumber, and most of the damaged parts had been pulled away.

A second pickup pulled into the lot and Bobby Barlow got out of the driver's side. He lumbered over, still limping a bit from his knee-replacement surgery a few weeks earlier. Colton found himself smiling, as if he was five years old again and his father had shown up at the father-son baseball game at school.

"Mornin'," Bobby said to his three sons. "Where do you need me?"

Luke waved at Colton. "Colton's in charge, so ask him."

Bobby turned to his oldest son. He looked a little uncomfortable, as if he'd rather ask anyone else on site what to do. But the other three Barlows were staring at Colton expectantly, so he cleared his throat and waved at the shop.

"We got most of the demo done," he said. "Luke and Mac are going to work on reconstructing the exterior wall. I was thinking you and I could rebuild the front counter."

"Sounds good. I've built a few cabinets over the years. Let's get started." Bobby unclipped a tape measure from his belt and walked into the empty store. He turned to Colton as he moved about the space. "You ever build a cabinet before?"

"Nope. Installed them, but never built one."

"It's not tough. Basically a big box. For one this long, though, you need to be sure you have enough interior support for the weight of the countertop. Now, are we making it the same as before?"

"I think that's the easiest option. That way, not too much changes inside the store."

"Ernie would like that. He hasn't changed a thing in this place for thirty years, and I don't expect him to go all crazy now. If it's the same, it's familiar, and that's going to make him more inclined to come back here."

"Then let's keep it the same," Colton said. Bobby called out some measurements, and Colton scribbled them onto a small pad of paper. Then they turned to the pile of fresh lumber sitting in the parking lot. Luke and Mac had set up a table saw on a couple of sawhorses repurposed into a worktable.

"Measure twice, cut once," Bobby said. He lifted one of the boards onto the table and stretched the tape measure along the side, marking where he was going to cut. "You want to cut?"

"Sure."

"Before you start," Bobby said, "make sure you adjust the blade height so the top of the blade is just above the board. It makes it more efficient."

Colton checked the blade, measuring it against the two-by-twelve, then brought down the blade guard. "Check."

"Be sure to keep your fingers far from the guard. I know it's there to protect you, but nothing's infallible. I like to keep my little finger against the fence when cutting something as wide as this. Helps guide the board and keep it all in place."

"Thanks." Colton did as his father instructed, feeding the board through the blade a little at a time. Bobby stood at the other end, helping guide the long piece of wood. They ripped several boards, one after another, working in concert. The plywood backer and top were cut next, then stacked to the side.

From time to time, Luke or Mac would glance over at them, but neither stepped in. The other two Barlows just kept to their own project, leaving Colton and Bobby alone. Other townspeople filtered into the space, lending a helping hand wherever it was needed, whether it was rebuilding the walls, or removing the damaged inventory or cleaning what could be salvaged. Before the little hand got past ten, almost two dozen people had shown up to help. Luke and Mac kept the extra helpers busy while Colton and Bobby worked on the counter.

Once the wood was cut, Colton and Bobby got to work assembling the counter base. "Let's drill the holes for the shelves now," Bobby said. "Easier to do it before assembly than to climb in there afterward. And that gives Ernie an option to move the shelves if he doesn't like the way we do it."

"All right. Let's make a template first," Colton said. "That way, they're all even."

"Good idea." Bobby nodded his approval, and Colton felt like a little kid who just got an A on a paper.

Colton tore off a piece of paper then measured out the right spacing for the holes. He held the paper against the board, and Bobby drilled the holes. When they were done, Bobby routed a groove a few inches above the bottom then held the first shelf steady while Colton screwed it in place.

"This bottom one should be set permanently in place," Bobby said. "Gives the whole cabinet more structural integrity. And by routing a groove for the shelf to fit into, we create an additional layer of support."

Colton helped his father repeat the process with the other side. As they worked together, filling in the center supports and creating the additional shelves, Colton began to anticipate Bobby's requests. They talked less and worked together more, developing a natural rhythm. The work filled the gaps in that awkward space between small talk and conversation.

A little while later Colton handed his father the last screw, and Bobby sank it into the plywood top. The laminate countertop would be delivered later, but for now the counter space was done. The two of them stepped back and assessed their handiwork.

The counter stood in the sun before them, eight feet long and smelling of freshly cut wood, a new beginning for Ernie Morris. But for Colton and Bobby Barlow, those few sheets of plywood were the start of something even more lasting. Something Colton had been searching for all his life, in those Christmases and birthdays and first days of school when he'd desperately wanted a father by his side.

Now he had him. Thirty years late, but that didn't matter anymore.

"Not bad," Bobby said, then reached out an arm and draped it across Colton's shoulders. For a second the embrace felt stiff, awkward, as Colton stood there, unsure of how to read this whole morning, the last few days, Bobby's distance.

"You know," Bobby went on, his arm still on Colton's shoulders, "there are some imperfections in this cabinet. Some would say it's not good enough, because it doesn't live up to the dream. But if you ask me, the knots in the wood and the nicks on the edge give it character. This piece is strong and solid and it's gonna last. It'll be here—" he met Colton's gaze, the mirror image of his own blue eyes "—for as long as you need it to be. You can depend on it."

Colton realized then that *this* was his father's way of bonding. With tools and wood and sawdust. "That's all I ask, Dad," he said. "That's all I need."

Bobby nodded, his eyes watering. "Me, too." A moment passed, Colton's throat tight, his heart full. Then his father gave him a hearty pat on the back. "Okay. Let's build something else...son."

Her father was not cooperating.

"I don't want to go home and rest," Ernie said as they left the hospital and got into Rachel's sedan. It was the same argument her father had given her since she came to pick him up that morning. The doctor had recommended he take it easy for a couple days, and that had set off a litany of protests from Ernie. "I don't want to spend one more damned day sitting in that house."

"But, Dad, you went through a lot last night and you should—"

"I should get back over to the store and see how bad the damage is. That's what I should do." Ernie put up a hand to cut off her objections. "I know I have spent a long time sitting at that kitchen table, having the longest pity party this side of the Mississippi. But I realized last night that I was just dragging you and the store and everyone around me down by doing that. I need to get back to work, Rachel."

"But, Dad, I don't..." She let out a long breath. "I don't think there's a shop to go back to. Harry said the damage was pretty extensive."

She hadn't wanted to tell her father that. She was afraid that if he knew the shop was gone, he would retreat to his cave again, and she'd never get him to leave. Maybe if she could keep him away until the insurance kicked in and everything was rebuilt...

"Then why are you taking the long way home?" her

father asked. "You know we're supposed to go straight down Main."

"I just think it's better if you wait—"

"Rachel Marie Morris, I am old enough to decide if I can handle seeing a little fire damage or not." Her father so rarely used her middle name or got stern that Rachel almost had to laugh. "So don't make my decisions for me, my darling daughter." His voice had softened, tempering the lecture.

"Dad, it's not a little fire damage. Harry said—"

"I heard Harry talking to you in the hall." Ernie reached out and covered her hand with his own. "And I appreciate you trying to keep the truth from me. I know you do it out of love. But isn't it about time this whole family stopped doing that with each other? And just faced the reality head-on?"

She braked at a stop sign and hung her head. Her father was right. For decades, none of them had talked about her mother's alcoholism. None of them had called her out on it. They'd made excuses and swept it under the rug, and when her mother got sick, her mother had played the same game, pretending the cirrhosis didn't exist until it was too late. In the year since, they'd tiptoed around their grief, as if ignoring it would ease the pain. But she was afraid, so afraid, that if she opened that door, the floodgates would burst. She was barely keeping her life under control as it was. "Dad, I can't do that. I can't…"

"Let me down?" His hand tightened on hers. "Because if that's what you think you did, let me tell you right now, you never did that."

She shook her head. Tears welled in her eyes. "I did. For too many years. I left you to take care of Mom and I shouldn't have. I just couldn't…couldn't see her like that."

"First of all, I loved your mother, loved her more than life itself, but she was a stubborn woman, and there wasn't anything you or I or God Himself could do to get her to listen. And second of all, I'm your father. It's my job to take those burdens on my shoulders so you don't have to. I've done a crappy job of it over the last year, and I'm sorry for that. I just got…lost."

"It's okay, Dad."

"If it's okay, then let's go see the store." He squeezed her hand again, and in his grip, she felt strength, determination. "Together."

"All right." She pressed on the gas pedal and made her way down Main Street toward the store. Maybe her father was more ready to see the damage than she expected. He was right; she shouldn't have to keep protecting him. He was a grown man, and one who had handled worse before.

"I really am sorry, Rachel," he said. "I left you to handle all this, and I never should have. And I'm sure as hell not leaving you to handle the rebuilding of the store. It's going to take some time, I know that, but—"

Her father cut off midsentence. Rachel followed his line of sight and gasped. The store, which she was sure would be all in ruins, was a hive of activity. The Barlows were there, building and cleaning, along with several other townspeople who had pitched in to help. There was a full Dumpster of charred lumber, but the new exterior wall was going into place, and she could see Colton and his father working on some repairs inside the store.

There was a lot of work left to be done, for sure, but the transformation was astounding.

She parked the car across the street, then she and her father got out. A table saw whined, punctuated by the pounding of a hammer. There was a low hum of voices, the occasional sprinkle of laughter. The sun was shining and the entire shop, while still half assembled, was taking on an air of a new beginning.

"Who did all this?" Ernie said.

"I don't know." As they crossed into the parking lot, Luke came up to them. His fiancée, Peyton, was beside him, along with a little girl wearing a bandanna and carrying a child-size hammer.

"Hey, Rachel. Ernie." Luke grinned. "Have you met my daughter, Madelyne?"

Rachel bent down to the little girl. "Hello, Madelyne. Are you helping today?"

The little girl nodded. "Uh-huh. Daddy's got me my own hammer. I'm gonna build a store."

Luke ruffled her hair. "Or at least part of one. Anyway, welcome to the madhouse."

"How…" Ernie turned and took in the busy scene. "When? Who…? I don't even know what to ask."

"Well, first of all, you're asking the wrong Barlow. This was all Colton's doing. He's the one who called us all and dragged us out of bed to put us to work." Luke pointed across the lot toward Colton, who was building a set of shelves with his father.

"Luke, why don't you show me what all you guys have been doing," her father said. "And Rachel, you go talk to Colton."

She arched a brow. Her father couldn't have been more obvious if he tried. But he walked off with Luke, leaving her to either tag along or do as he said. As she approached, Bobby wandered off, muttering something about going to get some more wood and nails, leaving her and Colton alone.

He looked so good, standing there in the sun, his face set with concentration as he measured and marked the shelving unit they had started. One of several they were working on, if the pile of cut wood beside him was any indication.

A faint dusting of sawdust covered his skin, powdered his dark hair and caught in the stubble on his cheeks. She thought of being in her bed with him last night, having his warm, long body against hers. It hadn't just been the lovemaking that she had enjoyed—because that had been outstanding—it had been the after, when Colton held her to his chest and pressed soft kisses to her temples. *That* was the man she was falling for—the man who would hold her in the dark then come here the next day and rebuild her father's shop without being asked.

And falling for him was a very dangerous proposition. He wasn't staying, and she wasn't sure where she was going. It was the worst possible time to get involved, to build a connection.

"What are you doing, Colton Barlow?" she asked.

He glanced up at her, and that lopsided smile she

had grown to love filled his face. "Making up for last night."

"Last night? That was…amazing." She blushed. Damn, she was like a schoolgirl.

He put down the tape measure and closed the distance between them. "I'm not talking about that part of last night. And I agree, yes, it was…incredible. I was talking about what happened to the shop. I…I didn't drive by soon enough or I would have seen the lightning strike, gotten your father out sooner. This—" he waved toward the pile of rubble filling the Dumpster "—wouldn't be like this if I had just been here at the right time."

"But you *were* here at the right time." She pressed a hand to his cheek. "You got my dad out safe and sound and got the fire department here fast enough to keep the entire building from going up. Not to mention, the whole block."

He looked away as if he was embarrassed by her praise. "I only did what anyone would have done."

"No, Colton, you did more. Much more." She released him, then looked around at the hive of activity. "I don't know how you got all this arranged and moving so fast. What about the insurance adjuster and paperwork and all that stuff?"

"I called Luke, and he called in a favor. There are some benefits to a small town. Like one insurance agent for everybody. We got Mike Simpson out of bed early this morning. He came over, did his analysis and took his pictures and is submitting the report today. Your dad should have his insurance money very soon."

"But then you did all this…" She waved toward the Dumpster, the wood, the supplies. "Did you pay for this yourself?"

He shrugged. "What's a Home Depot credit card for if you're not using it? Jack donated most of the supplies, and I filled in the gaps."

He'd done too much, Rachel thought, and she didn't know how to undo it. Everything her father had worked for, gone in a single night, until Colton came along and decided to make it right. "Colton, I can't let you do all this."

"Too late. It's done." He grinned. "Now, if you really want to thank me, then hold this end up while I fasten the board to the back."

She did as he asked, watching Colton work the screw gun to connect the shelf to the backer. He had done an incredible thing, and as much as she appreciated it, she was pretty sure there was some part of the story he was leaving out. And as much as her heart yearned to love him, her brain threw up a caution flag. She'd do well to listen.

She knew too well the damage that secrets and lies could do.

Chapter Eleven

There were few things in life that gave Bobby Barlow more joy than working with his sons. Even when they were little, he'd loved having the boys underfoot in the garage, or out in his workshop. Jack and Luke had followed in his footsteps, with Jack turning to wood-working and remodeling and Luke taking over the auto repair business, while Mac tinkered in his free time.

But working with Colton had been an entirely different experience. For one, the two of them didn't have decades of common language to draw from, like Bobby had with the other boys. For another, he was almost starting from scratch with Colton. For the ten thousandth time, regret filled Bobby that he hadn't been there during Colton's childhood. Would things have been different? Would Colton have lived here, been raised like one of the others? Or would they have a distant, difficult relationship, complicated by the miles apart and their different mothers?

He was proud of his sons, each and every one of them. Proud to be their father. But that didn't mean he didn't have a few million regrets about the kind of father he'd been.

And now there was Colton, who didn't seem to be in a hurry to leave town. A part of Bobby was happy— he really wanted to fill in the gaps of the last three decades. But as he talked to one neighbor after another during the rebuilding, and explained how Colton was related to the other boys, Bobby began to wonder if this whole thing was such a good idea. Maybe he shouldn't have come down here to help out. Maybe he shouldn't have drawn so much attention to the biggest mistake he'd ever made.

Della's Taurus pulled up and she got out of the car. They'd been married nearly thirty-five years now— just a few days from that landmark anniversary—but every time he saw her, his heart still leaped. She was curvy in all the right places, and though the red in her hair had dimmed a bit, she remained the sweet, loving, amazing woman he had married. He had been stupid when he'd been young, too scared of the prospect of *forever* to realize what he might have lost when he began that brief affair in Atlanta, but now, he knew he had hit the jackpot when it came to wives.

She was carrying a cloth grocery bag in one hand and a small cooler in the other. Bobby put down the drill he was using and crossed to her. "Here, let me get that," he said.

She giggled—even all these years later, she'd still giggle like a schoolgirl and for a moment he'd feel fifteen again—and gave him a quick kiss on the cheek. "Thank you, my knight in shining armor."

"I'm your knight in sawdust," he said, swiping some of the construction debris off the front of his T-shirt. "I wouldn't recommend getting too close."

"Oh, when has you being messy ever bothered me?" She swatted at some of the sawdust then gave him a second kiss. "I've brought some sandwiches and cookies for everyone. And a bunch of water bottles. It's hot out today."

"Thanks, honey. We can use it." He glanced over at the three boys, their heads together as they collaborated on something they were building. It was a nice sight, one that warmed his heart. Still, he worried about Della, about the ripples that were impacting her, the last woman to deserve this kind of thing. "Do you want to stay? You don't have to. I mean, we have this more or less under control."

"I…" She looked at her sons, gave them a little wave then returned her attention to Bobby. "I don't know what good I'd be. You know me and tools. I'm liable to break something before I fix it."

He saw Harry Washington heading their way. He liked the fire chief, but he could be a long-winded man, and the last thing Bobby wanted was to subject Della to a conversation about Colton. As much as possible, Bobby wanted to shield her from the subject. She'd done nothing wrong, yet he could see the neighbors even now, glancing between Colton and Della, whispering about the state of the Barlow marriage. His wife's reputation was tarnished merely by wearing his ring, and that wasn't something Bobby liked at all. "You don't have to stay," he said again.

"Okay." She laid a hand on his arm. "I have something else I need to do, anyway."

This was the third time this week that his wife had said something vague about where she was going and what she was doing. Bobby waved off Harry, signaling that he'd be back in a second, then left the food on the workbench and followed Della to her car. "Where are you going?"

She shrugged. "I have an appointment."

"With a...divorce lawyer?" He said the words as a joke, but frankly, ever since the truth had come out about his affair and the son that relationship had produced, Bobby had been worried Della would leave him. She'd be justified. What could he possibly say to make her stay? *Yes, the entire foundation of our marriage is a lie. But I never meant to hurt you. I still love you. I always have.*

She'd surely stop listening after the first sentence, and he couldn't blame her. They had barely talked about this whole thing in the days since she found out about Colton. Every time Bobby tried to get up the courage to broach the topic, his resolve faded again. What if Della said that she was done?

So he pretended the topic didn't exist and made stupid jokes because he was a total idiot six out of seven days a week.

Della didn't answer him until she reached her car. His heart damned near fractured waiting for her to tell him he was being silly. She got to the Taurus, put her back to it and crossed her arms over her chest. "I'm doing something for myself, Robert."

"Okay. Like…a facial or something?"

"No. Something bigger than that. I don't want to say anything until I figure out if this is what I want." She let out a sigh and toyed with her car keys. "This whole thing with Colton really threw me for a loop. Everything I thought I knew about us, about you, was based on a lie."

Bobby wished the ground would just open him up and eat him whole. The last thing he ever wanted to do was cause pain to the only woman he had ever loved. "I don't know how many ways I can say I'm sorry, Della. I was a moron. I didn't realize how good I had it until I almost lost you."

"You best keep that in mind, Robert Barlow." She wagged a finger at him. "Women like me don't come along every day."

"Trust me, I know that." He gave her a grin, hoping it would lighten her mood, but if anything the line in her lips tightened.

"I think…maybe it's time I stopped being Mom and wife and maid and cook. I think it's high time I did something for me."

"Uh…okay." He could feel it in his bones. This wasn't going to end well. His heart was already starting to break, and he readied a thousand pleading sentences in his head. "Della—"

"Stop." She put up a hand. "Just hear me out."

"Okay." He nodded.

"You did a terrible thing years ago. The worst thing you could have ever done. And even though it's more than thirty years in the past, it's only a few days in the past for me. I'm still dealing with it and trying to see my way back to loving you."

Damn it. "Della—"

"Let me finish, *please*." She let out a breath and stared down at the keys in her palm. "I'll get there, Bobby, but it's going to take me some time. As for Colton, he's a wonderful young man, and I welcome him into our family. He did nothing wrong, and it wasn't his fault how he came to be or who he was born to. We can't undo the last thirty years, but we can't pretend they didn't happen, either."

"I know that. I just want to make it easier on you." He ached to reach out to her, but she was holding herself stiff, in that way that told him that touching her would only make it worse.

"By ignoring a son who needs you, even if he's grown?" She shook her head. "No, Bobby. That's not the way to do it. We are going to have this family the same way we always have—out loud. We've never been quiet people, and I'll be damned if I'm going to let some busybodies make me feel like I can't keep my family just the way it is, warts and all."

That sounded good to Bobby. Except for the unspoken *but* he heard in her words. "Okay. We'll make

Colton feel as much a part of the family as the other boys."

"And at the same time, I am going to start carving out my own little corner. I need that, Bobby. My boys are grown, my husband is busy with his own things—"

"Della, don't do this." Dread churned in his stomach. He wanted to rewind the clock three decades, be a better father, a better husband, a better man. "God, please, don't—"

She put up a hand. "After thirty-five years, Robert Barlow, one would think you would have learned not to try to guess what a woman is thinking. Especially this woman."

"You're right, but…" He didn't finish the sentence. He needed to let her say what she was going to say. Putting it off wasn't going to make the words any easier to take. "Go ahead."

"It's time for *me*, Bobby. To figure out what I want and where I'm going to go from here. So my appointment is something to do with that. I don't know how it's going to work out, and I don't want to tell you about it because I want this decision to be entirely my own. Not Della the mother or Della the wife. Just me."

"Will you…" He let out a long breath. "Will you be home tonight?"

A smile crossed her face, and she pressed a hand to his cheek. "Of course. You aren't getting rid of me that easily. Now go back to helping your sons and don't worry so much. We're Barlows. We're going to be just fine."

Then Della got in her car and pulled away. Bobby

watched her go, until the taillights flickered and the car disappeared around a curve. He wasn't sure what Della had just told him. Didn't know whether to be sad or hopeful.

He loped back over to his sons and sat on over-turned buckets with them, eating sandwiches and drinking water, and praying for a miracle.

Colton knocked off for the day a little after six, as the sun began to sink in the sky and it got too dark to work safely. They cleaned up, then the three Barlow boys stood back to assess their progress. Bobby had gone home a little while earlier, but Luke and Mac had stayed, waving off Colton's offer to finish up on his own. They were good men, his brothers, and he was proud to be related to them.

"It's coming along nicely," Colton said.

"Yup. Glad Dad was here to make sure we did it right. He knows more than all of us put together." Luke let out a breath then turned to Mac. "Speaking of Dad, do you think he seemed a little…distracted today?"

Mac shrugged. "I don't know. Maybe. Or maybe he was just tired. This was a lot of work for him, and he's still recovering from his knee surgery."

"Yeah." Luke thought about that for a second longer. Didn't seem to come to a conclusion. He turned to his brothers and brightened. "Okay, well, I better get home."

"You do realize you look like a complete fool when you say that, don't you?" Mac said. "All grins and sighs. *Oh, I better get home.*"

"Hey, I have an amazing fiancée and daughter wait-ing for me. Of course I'm glad to get home. And you're the same way when it comes to Savannah, you big lug, so don't pretend you're any less *in love* than the rest of us."

"Colton's not in love. The only smart one in the fam-ily. We're all getting married, and he's still doing his own thing." Mac grinned. "Lucky stiff."

Luke scoffed. "I've seen the way he looks at Rachel Morris. And besides, look at what he did today. That's a man in love, mark my words."

"Hey, guys? I'm right here, you know," Colton said.

"Yeah, and you're a Barlow. Which means sometimes you need a wake-up call to see an amazing woman is right—" Luke pointed across the parking lot "—there."

Colton turned and saw Rachel standing there with a smile on her face. She was wearing jeans that hugged her thighs and outlined her amazing shape, and a pair of spaghetti strap tank tops, pink over white. He could see the pale pink straps of her bra beneath, and for some reason, it struck him as one of the sexiest things he'd ever seen. She had her hair down, loose around her shoulders, and he wanted nothing more than to bury his hands in those golden locks and kiss her senseless.

"See? Look at how he stares at her," Luke whispered to Mac. "How much you want to bet we have a fourth Barlow wedding in the near future?"

Mac thought a second. "Hundred bucks."

Luke laughed. "You must think Colton is made of stronger stuff than you or me."

"Again," Colton said, "I'm right here."

"That's right," Luke said. "You want in on this, too?"

Colton just laughed and shook his head then left his busybody brothers behind as he crossed to Rachel. "Hey," he said, because he didn't seem to have too many words in his head right now.

"Hey yourself." She smiled. Dazzling. Absolutely dazzling. "I managed to get my dad to stay home, but only with the promise that I would stop by and see how things are progressing."

So she'd come to check on the building, not to see him. He shouldn't be disappointed, but he was. "We got a lot done today. Do you want to do a walk-through with me? The power is still off, but it's light enough out to see pretty much everything we did today."

"Okay. Thanks." She followed along with him, stepping through the temporary door they had hung in the entry. It would be replaced with a new glass door tomorrow, but for now an old interior door was doing the trick.

Once they got inside, a wave of nerves choked up his throat. He'd done all this without permission or input, and suddenly Colton worried that he had gone too far. What if neither Rachel nor Ernie liked what Colton had done? What if Ernie wanted an entirely different design? Or what if Ernie wanted things exactly the same, and Colton had mangled the details?

He wanted Rachel to love the renovations. But the only way to find out if she did was to just show her and quit standing here like he'd lost his voice and his brains on the side of a highway.

"My dad and I rebuilt the counter," Colton said.

"The laminate should arrive tomorrow, and then that'll be done. We couldn't get the exact same pattern, but we found one that was close and has a more durable surface." He gestured to the left. "We hung shelves and pegboard behind the register, to give you more options for last-minute purchase items. I thought if people could see the things there while they were paying, they might add on to their order."

Rachel nodded. "That's a great idea. The whole thing is great, Colton."

He liked that she was pleased with the changes. He liked it more than he wanted to admit. Mac and Luke were right—Colton had a thing for Rachel Morris, and he suspected it wasn't a feeling that was going to go away anytime soon. It had started in this very shop, and had been quadrupled by the time they had spent together, that amazing night at her place and now this, watching her reaction to the work he had done on her father's store.

"Did I tell you that the shelves are all adjustable?" Colton went on. "So you can change the height of them to accommodate inventory changes." He stepped over a pile of lumber and put out a hand for her.

She could have gotten over the wood on her own, but she put her hand in his, anyway. "This is all fabulous."

He gestured toward the eastern wall. "We had to tear that entire wall down and rebuild it from scratch. The siding and Sheetrock should go up tomorrow, but for now we have a tarp over it, in case it rains."

"It all looks great. I can't believe how much you got done."

Colton kept moving, but didn't let go of her hand. "We also took the liberty of rebuilding the break room. The way it was set up before—"

"You couldn't open the door without hitting the table." She spun in the new space. It seemed bigger, brighter, even though it was the same square footage, just rearranged. The new design made so much more sense, she didn't know why no one had thought to do this before. "So you moved the door? And relocated the shelving to the far wall? Oh, and the counter is L-shaped now, instead of just one long piece."

"I was worried about changing it. I wasn't sure your dad would approve."

"Actually, my dad has wanted to do that for years. It's like you read his mind." She smiled at him. "Another great job here."

"No problem." He cleared his throat as if the praise embarrassed him. "Anyway, tomorrow we're going to run another waterline so you can have an ice-maker refrigerator."

They stood in the dim interior of the room where Rachel had eaten dozens of sandwiches, or sat beside her father while he drew pictures to keep his little girl occupied on the Saturdays she'd gone to work with him. It was going to be a slightly different, but much more efficient space. She could already see how much better it was going to work out, and how much easier it would make days at the shop. Not to mention the forethought and details Colton had put into the front of the store, with the adjustable shelves, the flexible space behind the counter.

Colton, it seemed, had thought of everything. He'd matched so much of the original store, it was as if he'd been the one working here for the last year. "How did you come up with all of this? I mean, you've only been in the store once. It's like you divined all the issues we've had over the years and fixed them in one fell swoop."

He shrugged. "I didn't sleep last night. I came down here, did a walk-through to assess the damage then went back to my room and drew up some plans. I'm no carpenter, so thankfully my father and brothers helped me fine-tune it. And I'm sorry not everything is here or in place yet. Some things we had to wait on and—"

She rose on her tiptoes and placed a kiss against his lips. "Thank you."

He seemed surprised, but a smile crossed his face and he kissed her back. "Oh, Rachel, you don't have to thank me."

"I do indeed. You went above and beyond, Colton." She curved into his chest and wrapped her arms around his back. He smelled of fresh-cut wood and fall air, and she thought she'd never before known a man to give as much as Colton Barlow had, to people who were essentially strangers. "You really know what matters most to people and just…do it. No wonder you're always saving lives."

He shook his head, as if he disagreed, then wrapped her in his arms, and when his gaze connected with hers, she felt as though she was in a fantasy world where everything was going to be just fine. That all these challenges and problems would pass in a blink. "I just hope with all the changes, and the new start, it's enough to get your dad back to work. So then you can go back to what *you* want to do."

She stepped out of his arms and let out a sigh. There was the real world again, intruding like an unwanted party guest. "I don't know if it's as simple as that."

"Of course it is." Colton gave her a grin. "Besides, I hear there's a girl named Ginny who really wants you to plan her wedding."

"How do you know that?"

"It's a small town, remember? And her fiancé was one of the ones who pitched in today. She came and brought him a soda and went on and on about how this was such bad timing, because she really wanted you to be free to, and I quote, 'plan the pinkest wedding this county has ever seen.'"

Rachel laughed. "That is what Ginny wants. And it would be the kind of big, bold, over-the-top wedding that would make the papers and give my business a nice boost of publicity."

"So…what's stopping you?"

The sun was nearly gone now, and the shop was almost too dark to see inside. It had become a space filled with shadows, instead of the new opportunities she had seen earlier when the sky was still light. "I don't want to leave my father shorthanded."

He snorted. "Is that all it is?"

She spun back toward him. "What do you mean?"

"I think you're afraid."

She scoffed. Colton didn't know anything about her. He couldn't tell her how she was feeling. Even if deep down she knew he was a little—okay, a lot—right. But still she protested, because admitting the truth meant dealing with the truth. "I'm not afraid of anything."

"You should be." He paused a beat. "Because I am."

That surprised her. This powerful man, who could rescue people and save buildings and transform a shell of a store, was scared? "Come on. You? What could you possibly be afraid of?"

He took a step closer, winnowing the space between them to almost nothing. A moment passed, another, and outside the streetlights came on and cast a shaft of gold down the center of the store. "I'm afraid of falling for you and falling for this town and changing my entire life to be here."

He was really falling for her? Those words had been more than just something said in the heat of the moment last night? And he was thinking about staying here?

"That's not so scary." She said those words, but inside her heart was pounding, and her pulse was racing. Because the whole idea scared the hell out of her, too. The very thing she never thought existed—a happy ending for herself—could be standing right before her, in this six-foot-two firefighter who gave more of himself than anyone she'd ever met.

"It is for me." He took her hands in his. "I told myself I was happy with my life in Atlanta. But that was a lie. And admitting that means I need to make a change."

"A change to Stone Gap?" She hoped so. Good Lord, did she hope so.

"Maybe. It depends on…a couple of things."

Once again, she got the sense that there was a wall between herself and Colton, something he wasn't sharing with her. Their relationship was new, barely a week old, but still, after last night… "Well, you've already got a job offer and a reputation as a hero, so—"

He spun away. "That is not what I want people to think of me."

"Why not? That's what you are. Running into a burning building and rescuing my father? That's heroic and amazing. I'm sure you did that dozens of times in Atlanta. Stone Gap would be lucky to have a firefighter like you on the force."

He cursed and kept his back to her. "I'm not what you think I am, Rachel. I'm not even close."

"Come on, no need to be modest. You did a great thing—"

He wheeled around, and even in the dim interior, she could see the flash in his eyes, hear the anger in his voice. "Is it a great thing to be responsible for two of your friends dying? For getting in that building too damned late, then watching the beams come down and seeing the fire follow like an angry, hungry beast, and then hearing the screams of terrified men? Then, the worst part of all, the part that haunts my dreams. Hearing the screams…stop." He shook his head and cursed again. "I'm not a hero. So quit saying that."

He stalked out of the break room. She waited a moment, taking in everything he'd just said, then followed and found him in the front part of the shop, staring out at the quiet street. No wonder Colton hadn't wanted to talk about his career as a firefighter. She couldn't even begin to imagine how painful and difficult something like that had been, to see and hear your friends die and know you were powerless to stop it.

But to her, that made him *more* of a hero, not less. Because he *had* tried, even when the odds were against him. He'd fought for the lives of others. And what's more, he had stayed with the fire department, and kept on running into burning buildings, like her father's store. That was a hero, whether Colton saw the truth or not. Rachel put a hand on his back. Colton tensed, but didn't move away.

"Colton, things like this happen," she said softly. "You can't save everyone."

"I *should* have saved them, Rachel. I could have. If only I'd been faster, faster into my gear, faster off the truck, faster into the building. I only needed a minute, maybe two, and I could have saved them." His voice was thick, the words catching in his throat. "But I wasn't, and they died, and I…I haven't been the same since."

"I'm sorry," she whispered and pressed her cheek to his back. She could feel the pain in his muscles, hear it in his voice. The regrets lay heavy on Colton Barlow, and he couldn't seem to find a way to let go of them.

"I can't work here," he said. "What if it happens again? In a town this small, everyone knows everyone. And if a guy dies because I'm not fast enough—"

"Stop that." She came around in front of him and

met his gaze. "Stop planning for things that you don't know are going to happen. Stop creating situations that may never exist. Accidents happen, whether you work for a fire department or a fast-food place. You can't predict when or where or how. And you can't beat yourself up for simply doing your job."

"If I was doing my job, they would have been alive."

"You *were* doing your job, Colton. And sometimes, that job doesn't turn out the way you want it to."

He shook his head, still not hearing her, not believing her. "Rachel, just stop trying to make me into something I'm not."

"You *are* a hero, Colton, whether you accept it or not. It's *you* that has to stop trying to make yourself into something that you aren't." She cupped his face and met his gaze. His eyes were dark clouds, filled with pain, regret and disbelief in her words, in himself. "You're not a failure. You're a good man who went through a terrible loss."

The wall in his eyes bounced the words away. Whatever demons Colton was facing were not going to be solved with one conversation in a dark, half-constructed shop. "Come on, let's go for a walk," she said.

"A walk?"

"I never did finish the twenty-five-cent tour," she said, taking his hand before he could argue. "And there's something I want you to see."

Chapter Twelve

Colton was tempted to turn around and tell Rachel to forget it, but her hand grasped his firmly and left no room for argument. They started walking down Main Street, just as the moon was rising in the sky and dappling the streets with pale white.

"So, what are we going to see?" he asked, because it was easier to concentrate on the walk they were taking through the darkened streets than on the shadows that dogged him still. It was as if his friends were following him, reminding him with every step that he couldn't escape his past.

"You'll find out when we get there." She shot him a mischievous grin then turned right onto Berry Lane, and then a few minutes later a left onto Mulberry Avenue. It was the neighborhood of berries, apparently, because he saw a Strawberry Drive and a Raspberry Lane on either side of them, and they had passed a Blueberry Drive a second ago.

"You're acting like a woman of mystery tonight," he said. "I like it."

Even in the light from the street lamps, he could see her blush. "One more street," she said, and they turned onto Blackberry Lane.

The houses here were all squat bungalows, with scrappy yards and pastel paint jobs. He could smell the ocean, hear its soft song, just beyond the trees. Sand gritted under his shoes as they walked, mixed with crushed shells that sparkled in the moonlight.

Rachel stopped in front of a sunflower-yellow house with white shutters. A swing sat in the front yard, drifting a bit in the breeze off the water. Somewhere in the distance, a dog barked and a boat motored across the sea.

"Okay, so here's the next part of the tour." She cleared her throat then took a serious stance and tone. "Stone Gap is a town rich in history. It was settled long ago, soon after the Pilgrims colonized New England. It took a while to get its name, but it's always been a special place, filled with its share of legends and stories."

Colton chuckled. "That's part and parcel of living in the South. I think all the Spanish moss inspires people to make up mythical tales."

"I agree. But this particular story is true. I know this, because I went to school with Arnie Teague, who is a direct descendant of the family that used to live in this house."

He looked past her at the bright bungalow. "Cute little house, though a bit yellow for my tastes."

"It wasn't always that color. Back in the day, it was the only house here. The Teagues owned this entire section of Stone Gap, in fact."

"Judging by the street names here, they were big fans of fruit?" He liked Tour Guide Rachel, with her serious stone-and-stern face.

"That's how they made most of their income. Winona Teague grew all kinds of berries here, canned them and offered them for sale, locally and, later, up the coast, sending the orders off with her husband, who was a ship's captain. The berries sold like wildfire, because they were rumored to make people fall in love. A little jam on a sweetheart's toast in the morning, and wham, a proposal would come by the end of the day."

"Clever marketing or truth?"

"Maybe a little of both." Rachel gestured toward a bench a few feet away. They walked down and took a seat, facing the little yellow house. A cat darted out of the shadows and under the bench, then wound its way between their legs. Rachel bent down and patted the cat, a scrawny orange tiger. "Winona's husband, Charles, loved her to death. Would have done anything for her. But he was a sailor, so he was away more often than he was here.

"One winter Charles had to make an unexpected trip. A delivery, I think, for a local merchant who wanted to get his goods up north. The weather was bad, but Charles needed the money, so he set sail. The storm kicked up, and several sailors returned home early. But not Charles."

The cat jumped over Rachel's lap and settled itself between them. Colton scratched the fur ball behind its ears, and it leaned into him with a purr. Colton barely noticed.

"A week passed," Rachel went on. "Another. A third. A month. Winona was inconsolable. As time passed and there was no word or sign of her beloved husband, her precious berries grew overgrown, and either rotted or were consumed by birds. The thing she loved most to do was forgotten, and the canning jars grew dusty. She spent more and more time inside that little house, weeping for a man she would never see again."

"And this story is supposed to make me feel better?"

Rachel smiled then put up a hand. "Just wait. After two months of this, Winona realized her appetite was gone, not because she was grieving, but because she was pregnant. The baby that she and Charles had prayed to have was finally on its way, but Charles wasn't here. Everyone told her to move on, forget her husband and start her life anew. She was a pregnant widow, and she would do well to find another husband. This was decades ago, remember, and women didn't have many options or life insurance plans."

"That had to be tough."

"But Winona was tougher," Rachel said. "She decided to believe that Charles was still alive and that he would come back to her. So she got back to living as if he was. She tended to the berries, canned the jams and jellies, cleaned her house and painted it a bright yellow color, so that he could see it from the ocean. She wanted to be sure that he had a beacon to guide him home."

"And what did the rest of Stone Gap think?"

"They thought she was crazy. They told her she should accept reality and let go of the impossible. Move on and quit believing in what wasn't real." Rachel's voice was quiet, dark, carrying a spell as the tale wove between them. "But she refused to listen. Every day, she'd dress in her prettiest dress, do her hair the way Charles liked it and make a dinner that he would enjoy. In between, she grew her berries and canned, and made enough money to keep up with the property and the taxes."

He was completely hooked on the story. He wanted to know more, to hear how it ended. The cat had fallen asleep, its tail twitching against his back from time to time, but Colton kept on rubbing the cat's head, his attention fixed on Rachel's words. "How long did she do this for?"

"Five months and two weeks. The baby was nearly here, and still Winona refused to let any other men court her or to give up on the dream of Charles coming home. One night there was a terrible storm, more terrible than the one that Charles's ship had disappeared in. Winona went into labor, alone in that little house, so sure she was going to lose her baby. For the first time in the months since her husband disappeared, Winona gave up on ever seeing him again. She was certain that she and her child would die that night, and she accepted that fact, because she knew they would be reunited with Charles. Maybe, she thought, this was what God intended for her and their child."

"This better have a happy ending, Rachel. I'm starting to get depressed." Seriously, thought Colton. He wasn't quite sure how Rachel saw this as a good way to pass the evening, not to mention help him see through the despair plaguing him. He might need to ask for his money back on the twenty-five-cent tour.

Rachel laughed. "Hold your horses, cowboy. The storm raged on, with the wind howling outside and beating up the little yellow house with branches and rain. Lightning flashed as bright as sunshine, over and over. And just as the baby was about to crown, the door burst open, and there, standing in the doorway, soaking wet and with a beard reaching his chest, was Charles."

"No way. Where was he all this time?"

"He'd wrecked on one of the barrier islands off North Carolina. It took him months to build a boat big enough and strong enough to get him back to his beloved Winona. But he'd done it, and just in time to help deliver his son."

It was a story that left even Colton a little choked up, but as touched as he was, no way was he willing to admit he had a couple of tears in his eyes.

"Charles said it was the bright yellow paint that got him back to the right place. As he neared the coast, he could see the house through the lightning, so he set his course and kept on going until he reached home. He knew Winona would never give up on him, so he never gave up on her." Rachel smiled, a soft, sweet look that touched her eyes.

"That and eating all that magic love jam."

She laughed. "Yeah, maybe that, too. But the point of the story, and the reason people still tell it to this day, is that it should remind you that all is never lost. That there's always hope for a new beginning, for a new start."

He knew what she meant. That just because he had watched a tragedy unfold before his eyes, powerless to stop it, didn't mean that he wasn't a good firefighter. Didn't mean he couldn't take this job in Stone Gap and find a new life here. Maybe with Rachel. Maybe in some little yellow house on the water with berries growing in the yard and the ocean breeze drifting in through the windows.

A part of him really wanted that. Could even picture it, seeing Rachel standing in that yard, waiting for him to come home. But then he reminded himself that dreaming of a new future and actually having it were two different things. It was entirely possible that Harry would rescind the job offer once Colton told him about Willis and Foster. Then Colton would have to go back to Atlanta, back to the small brick building where the other men gave him those looks of pity and sympathy, and where every corner held a memory of the friends he had lost.

He could go back there, but where would that leave Rachel? He thought of the little hardware store, and knew she intended to go right back to working behind that counter instead of pursuing her own dreams.

"I'm not the only one who should remember the lessons from Winona and Charles," Colton said.

"What do you mean?"

He sat on the bench, his arm draped on the back, fingers brushing against her shoulder. The cat stirred in its sleep but didn't move, like a furry wall between them. "You have a chance at a new start, Rachel, once the shop reopens and your dad goes back to work, yet you keep dodging the answer of whether you are going to take it."

"I'm not dodging anything. I'm just helping my dad."

"Which is noble and wonderful. And which is what you have been doing for a year now, while the business you started withers away."

"There are only so many hours in the day, Colton." She scowled. "I couldn't keep both going."

"Couldn't? Or chose not to?"

She spun toward him. "What are you talking about?"

"You could have hired someone part-time for the hardware shop. Or worked at night on the wedding planning business."

"Easier said than done." She blew her bangs out of her face. "The shop has been struggling financially. I couldn't afford to hire someone else to work there. I barely took a paycheck myself all year."

This was where it got difficult. Where Colton had to say the things to her that he was pretty sure she already knew, but hadn't acknowledged. Things he was pretty damned sure he should also say to himself, but it was far easier to lecture Rachel than to face the same truths himself. "Don't you think you could have asked any of the dozens of people in this town who showed up throughout the day today to help rebuild, to take a shift or two for free? All I heard from the folks of Stone Gap was what a great guy your dad was and how they were more than willing to do what it took to help him get back on his feet. All you would have had to do was ask, Rachel, and I bet they would have lined up to help."

She shook her head. "It's not that simple."

"Why not?"

"Because it had to be me. Because I owed him." She jerked to her feet, scaring the cat. It jumped from the bench with an angry yowl and disappeared into the woods. "You don't understand, Colton, so stop pretending you do."

"If anyone in this world understands owing people, it's me." Colton crossed to her and took her hands in his. "We're so much alike, Rachel. Both of us trying to make up for mistakes we didn't even make."

She shook her head and tugged her hands out of his, putting distance between them again. The ocean whooshed in and out, like one of those white noise machines playing behind them. But it didn't ease the stress in Rachel's face.

"But *I* did make this mistake." Her voice was soft, broken. "I ran away when I should have stayed. I just couldn't…couldn't handle my mother another day. She drank and she got mean and she was so much to take care of. I was young and selfish and just wanted… space."

He could understand that. There were many days

when he was younger when he'd wanted to just leave town and not be responsible for his mother and sister. He'd wished he didn't have to be the "man" of the house and he could have just been an ordinary kid. "There's nothing wrong with that. We've all had those moments."

"But I left my father to deal with her. And when she got sick, my dad did everything alone, instead of telling me. He wanted me to keep working at my business, to pursue my career. By the time I found out…it was too late." She bit her lip and swiped at the tears welling in her eyes. "The least I could do for him was to run that shop while he grieved for however long it took."

"And put your own life on hold."

"I…I had to." Now the tears in her eyes brimmed and spilled over. Colton reached up and caught them on his thumb, wiping them away.

"How long are you going to let fear run you, Rachel?" he said.

"I'm…I'm not afraid." The words wobbled, and he knew he'd hit a truth.

"Oh, honey, you are. And that's totally okay." He drew her into his arms, not caring that her tears dampened his shirt. Colton was a man used to rescuing people. And once again, he couldn't rescue this one. If Rachel wanted the life she deserved—the life she had walked away from a year ago—she was going to have to be the one to go out there and get it.

There was probably a message in there for him, too, but he was going to have to shelve that for now.

"Take a chance," he whispered against her. "Take that leap."

She held on to him for a long time while the ocean crashed against the shore and the little yellow house stood bright and determined under the moon. "I wish I could, Colton," she said.

Then she walked away. He let her go, because he knew that until he was ready to take his own advice, he was never going to have the right words to convince Rachel to do the same.

Rachel woke up Saturday morning and lay in bed for a long time, staring at the ceiling. She missed Colton. Her hand snaked across the empty space beside her, but found only cold sheets. She'd dreamed about him, a dream so vivid, it seemed as if he should be here.

But he wasn't.

And a lot of that was her fault. He tried to get close to her, and she pushed him away. She kept undermining the very thing she wanted.

He was an incredible man. Considerate, loving, giving. He'd rushed in there and saved her father when another person might have run from the flames. He'd gone and single-handedly spearheaded the rebuilding of her father's store, and for no other reason than to help him. And he had made love to her in a way that had left her breathless and feeling like the most treasured woman on the planet.

All of which terrified her. How many years had she been planning weddings and dreaming of the very same happy ending for herself? Now that she had finally met a man who could fit the image she'd long wished for herself, she was afraid it would all pop, like a balloon.

Either way, she needed to focus on her father for now. Colton Barlow—and all he represented and all the questions he raised in her heart—would have to wait. Okay, so maybe she was making excuses, but she really didn't want to answer the questions that Colton had asked her last night.

She swung her feet over the bed and got up before she was tempted to lie there another second. A few minutes later she had showered, changed into old jeans and a T-shirt and pulled on some sneakers. She swept her hair into a ponytail and grabbed a granola bar and a water bottle on her way out the door. A little past seven, she pulled into her father's driveway and knocked on the door.

To her surprise, her dad opened the door. For almost a year, she'd knocked and gotten no response, and always ended up letting herself in. But there was her dad on the other side of the door, already dressed, his hair combed, his face shaved and a hot cup of coffee in his free hand. "Good morning."

She blinked. "Wow. You're up and ready, Dad?"

"Yup. Figured it was about time I got my act together."

"Are you feeling okay? Shouldn't you be resting—"

He put up a hand to cut off her words. "I feel fine. And I'm going to feel a lot better when I get out of here and over to the store. Sun's been up for thirty minutes already, and time's a-wastin'."

She laughed. This was the father she remembered, the can-do man who would work all day and then take her out in the yard to play catch or build a birdhouse. In her memory, her dad was tireless, a superhero she could always count on. "Okay, but what about breakfast?" She started to brush past him. "I can make some eggs and toast—"

"Already ate. I left you a plate on the stove. But eat fast, will you? I want to get down there as soon as I can."

Rachel turned to her father. "Who are you?"

His gaze softened, and a smile filled his face. "The dad you used to have."

That made Rachel's eyes water. Good Lord, she had cried more in the last few days than in the last year. She drew her father into a tight hug and said a silent prayer of thanks.

He patted her back. "Okay, okay. Enough of this before we turn into weeping willows. Eat your breakfast and we'll go."

She took a seat at the table. The roles had reversed, she realized, when her father put a plate before her and poured her a cup of coffee. Maybe her father was more ready to go back to his life than she thought.

How long are you going to let fear run you?

Was Colton right? Was she avoiding her business because she was afraid? Afraid that it had sat by the wayside for too long and may never recover?

Yet another set of questions she was not going to answer today. Or at least not right now.

Her father sat down across from her and sipped at

his coffee. "Before we leave, I wanted to talk to you about your mother. I know you've been bothered by what happened last year. And I just didn't talk about it, no matter how many times you tried to bring it up."

"It's a painful subject, Dad. It's okay."

"No, it's not okay." He let out a long sigh. "Not talking about the painful subjects is how we got to this place. With me sitting at the kitchen table, working on the same crossword puzzle all damned day. And with your mother, getting to the point where the cirrhosis was irreversible before she told us about it."

Rachel fiddled with her toast. "Maybe because we all perfected that over the years. Not talking about her drinking, not talking about how she had changed."

"Acting like if we pretended it didn't exist, it would stop being a problem?"

Rachel nodded. "Yeah."

"I loved your mother, Rachel. Loved her more than I can even say. But I failed her. I didn't stop her. I couldn't stop her. I tried, Lord knows I tried. Three times, I put her into rehab."

Rachel had never known that. She'd always thought her father had looked the other way, ignoring the truth for years. "You did?"

"When you were away at school. I thought maybe she'd get clean and we could have some semblance of family life. But every time, she'd come home and start again. It was as if she couldn't shake those demons, no matter how hard she tried."

"She was stuck in a rut, too scared to climb out of it." Gee, who did that sound like? Rachel realized she was doing the same thing, only she was using the shop instead of alcohol as a reason not to move forward. Except moving forward was a lot easier to think about than it was to do.

"I guess that's what kept me in this house for a year." Her father sighed. "I always felt like I had let your mother down. If I had tried harder or pushed her more…"

"We both should have, Dad," she said. The sunshine-shaped clock in the kitchen ticked past the hour, as it had for most of Rachel's life. So many things in this kitchen had stayed the same, stuck in a time warp. Her mother hadn't changed anything, not the stoneware pattern or the curtains in the window. Everything the same, day after day. "Honestly, I don't know if anything we could have done would have made a difference. She was the one who had to want a change, and we couldn't force that. Only encourage and support it."

"You're right, but that's a hard truth to accept," he said. "Maybe we all just needed to try harder."

"And maybe I shouldn't have gone away to school or worked so hard and left you to deal with all this." She sighed.

"I don't blame you, honey, for staying at school and working all the time. You saved yourself, and you have to do that."

She covered her father's hand with her own. "I did it at the expense of you. That's not right."

"It's exactly right." He patted the back of her hand and his eyes softened. "What do they tell you on the airplane? Put the oxygen mask on yourself before you put it on someone else. You saved yourself, and got yourself out of this situation so that you could grow up and be happy and healthy. And when you were strong enough, you came back and saved me."

She thought of the last year, of all the time and energy she had given to the man who had scared the monsters out of her childhood closet and taught her how to fish. Hours she would gladly give again and again.

He drew her into his arms. His cheek was smooth, scented with the familiar cologne she'd known all her life. His hug was firm and solid and comforting. "I love you, too. All the way to the moon…"

"And back," she whispered. "All the way back."

Chapter Thirteen

Colton stood in Harry Washington's office on the second floor of the brick building housing the Stone Gap Fire Department at an ungodly early hour on Saturday morning. Harry was eating a glazed donut and sipping from a giant coffee mug.

Harry had called last night and asked him to come by and meet before reconstruction got underway for the day at the hardware store. Harry had said they needed to talk before the sun got too high in the sky and ruined the day for man and beast. He gestured toward the seat opposite his desk and waited for Colton to take a seat. "Coffee?"

"No, sir. I'm good. Thank you."

"I can't start the day without a caffeine drip. My wife keeps trying to sneak decaf into my cup. Says I'm too high-strung," he scoffed. "You know what makes me high-strung? Drinking decaf. Waste of hot water, I say."

Colton chuckled. "I agree."

Harry leaned back in his chair and put his feet up on the desk. "So, you going to start with the department as soon as you can settle your affairs in Atlanta? Because I'm a man short, and you're just the firefighter I need to fill some empty boots."

Colton had thought about Harry's job offer most of the night. He'd tossed and turned, thinking about Willis and Foster, thinking about the mistakes he had made, the moves he wished he could do over and the regrets that hung heavy on his shoulders. Every thought circled back to the same thing—one of the last things Rachel had said to him yesterday.

There's always hope for a new beginning, for a new start.

Hope. An emotion he hadn't allowed himself to have in a very long time. Maybe he needed to start looking forward, instead of wallowing in a past he couldn't change. But first he needed to be honest with Harry Washington, so that if he did come to work at the Stone Gap Fire Department, it was with a clean slate.

"There's something you should know first, sir," Colton said. "And if it changes everything, I understand."

Harry dropped his feet to the floor and leaned forward. "Okay. Shoot."

Colton ran a hand through his hair and let out a breath. Even now, months later, talking about that night was akin to dragging a fish hook up his throat. "About six months ago, I…I lost two of my guys. I was the incident commander, and this was one of my first big fires. We got the call at 1320, rolled out at 1326 and pulled up on scene at 1338." All those details didn't matter, but somehow, delivering the information like an incident report made it easier for Colton to talk. "We secured a water supply, and I assigned Engine 4 to ventilation, keeping Engine 3 on fire attack. The building was almost fully engulfed before we got there. Access was impeded by an adjacent construction site."

Harry just listened, nodding once or twice. Colton went on, the words coming slower now. "I had a lot to assess when I first got on scene, a lot of pieces to set into place, you know?" How could he describe how overwhelmed he felt? Even though he had almost eight years of experience with the department, that first time when it was all on his shoulders—

Colton cleared his throat. "The building was a known location for transients. We had a report of a man trapped inside, and at 1358, I sent two of my most experienced guys in to attempt a rescue. Soon after they entered the building, the winds shifted, which forced the fire into the location where my men had gone. The flames had already leaped to the second floor, and—" Colton paused, forced the words out of his throat "—there was a catastrophic failure of the roof. My men were trapped under the debris. Engine 3 attempted an extraction, but—" He shook his head and let out a curse. He could see it now, the falling timbers, the way the fire chased behind, eager and hungry. The screams, oh, God, the screams. Colton had to struggle to keep his composure, to breathe. To speak. "I'm sorry, sir. The two men were DOS and I—"

"What were their names?" Harry said, his voice quiet.

"Sir?"

"What were the names of the men you lost?"

"David Willis and Richard Foster." He hadn't spoken their full names since the incident. As soon as he did, he could see David's wide grin, hear Richard's deep laughter. He could see them raising a beer at the Pint & Slice after a hard day on the job, hear them teasing him about his terrible cooking skills. As soon as Colton said their names aloud, they were alive again in his head, and that made the loss sting ten times more.

Harry nodded. "You write those names on the inside of your helmet, Barlow. Write David Willis and Richard Foster in big letters so you see their names every time you turn out. You remember them, son, and you remember that you are only human, and try as you might, you won't be able to save them all. You'll save the ones you can and remember the ones you can't."

Colton swallowed hard. "Yes, sir."

Harry leaned forward and crossed his hands on the desk before him. "When I was two years into this job, I lost a man. His name was Joe Dunlap. I've never forgotten that, and never forgotten him. His name is written inside my helmet, inside my coat and inside here." He leaned back and pulled open the center drawer of his desk. "He's my DOS, Barlow, but he's never going to be dead in here." Harry smacked at the space above his heart. "That's what keeps us from getting burned out. From getting to the point where we don't care. It's what gives you heart. And that's the kind of man I want in my department. One with heart."

"Sir, are you sure—"

"I saw you out there, rebuilding Ernie Morris's place with your bare hands. You didn't do it because he was going to give you a lifetime supply of fishing tackle—though if he does, I want in on that action." Harry grinned. "You did it because you have heart. Soul. That's why I don't give a crap about your résumé, Barlow. I don't care what's on a piece of paper or on an incident report. I care about what's inside the man. And what's inside you is exactly what I want to hire." Harry got to his feet and put out a hand. "So… what size uniform should I order?"

There was a definite spring in her dad's step as he headed out to Rachel's car later that morning, as if a weight had been lifted from both of them by finally talking about the subjects they had avoided for years. Maybe there was something to this facing your fears thing that Colton kept urging her to do.

In the car, they chatted about the work Colton had done the day before on the short ride over to the shop. As Rachel turned onto Main Street, she stopped dead. "Oh, my God. There's got to be fifty people there, helping."

Her father's eyes filled as he took in the dozens of parked cars, the multitude of people working on the job site, as busy as bees in a hive. "All these people? Helping me?"

"It looks like that, yes." A lump formed in Rachel's throat. She'd known Stone Gap was filled with good folks, but this many? Being this generous? To her dad? It was overwhelming and touching. And wonderful.

"Well, then, let's get to work," her father said. "Best thing I can do is open up the store as soon as possible, and thank everyone by being ready to help someone catch the biggest fish at this year's derby."

Rachel parked, and the two of them headed toward the store, her dad moving faster and with more eagerness than she had seen in a long time. It was good to see her father so excited about his business again, as if this setback had recharged him, rather than added to his despair. She hurried to keep up with her dad, then slowed her step as she neared the center of the construction site.

Colton stood in the middle of the parking lot, a pad of paper in his hands and a circle of people around him, waiting for him to dispense directions. He was wearing jeans and another button-down shirt, with the sleeves rolled up. The morning breeze ruffled his dark hair.

Dad leaned into Rachel. "That man's a keeper, I'm telling you."

"You might just be right about that, Dad."

"I'm your dad, I'm right about everything." He winked then strode forward and into the crowd. He grabbed Colton, gave him a quick hug and thanked him for his help. "Now, what do you want me to do?"

Colton greeted her father with a clap on the shoulder. "Morning, Ernie. Nice to see you here and glad you want to help. If you could direct people inside, that would be great. We need help restocking the inventory that we saved, and figuring out what needs to be reordered."

"Can do. I know that shop like the back of my hand." He grinned. "Can't wait to get back in there."

Rachel watched her father head off to the shop and marveled at the change in him. She had all but given up hope that he would ever get back to his old self. She felt that lump in her throat again, and thought if she didn't get busy doing something, she was going to turn into a sobbing mess right here in the parking lot.

"You want something to do, don't you?" Colton said.

"How'd you know?"

He just grinned and took her hand. "Come on, help me sand these shelves."

She gave the long boards a dubious look. "I don't know anything about sanding shelves."

"Good thing I do." He handed her a rectangular block of sandpaper. "Go with the grain and keep your strokes even. Nothing too hard and fast, or you'll create a divot, and you don't want that."

"Divots are bad?" She gave him a teasing grin.

His gaze slid over her, hot and slow. "Depends on where they are."

"Yes, indeed. Some divots are very good."

"Maybe later," he murmured against her ear, sending her pulse racing, "we can explore some of the very, very good divots."

"Maybe, Colton. If you're good."

He chuckled. "I'm good. Very good."

That made her mind go down some very dark, very naked paths. "Uh, I should get to work on this before…" Before she did something crazy.

She took up a space at one end of the board, Colton at the other. She tried to concentrate on sanding, but every fiber of her being was aware of him, just a few feet away. Every once in a while, she caught the scent of his cologne, or saw him smile, and her heart did a little flip.

"So, how did you learn how to do all this stuff?" she asked, because if she didn't start making conversation, she was pretty sure she'd start kissing him.

"Actually, I didn't. Not until this week, anyway. I mean, I knew some basic stuff—my uncle Tank showed me how to do things like paint a wall and replace the washer in a faucet. But working with my dad…" He smiled. "It was great. Really great."

"I'm so glad. I'm happy things are going well for you."

"Actually, things are going really well all around." He stopped sanding and turned toward her. "You're looking at the newest member of the Stone Gap Fire Department."

"You took the job? That's great. That means you'll be staying in Stone Gap."

She should have been excited. Overjoyed. Instead, this weird little fissure of fear ran through her. Colton was staying in Stone Gap, which meant there was no excuse not to get involved with him. No excuse not to risk her heart.

Except...risk. Yeah, she wasn't big on that. In any area of her life.

"So I was thinking..." Colton started to say, when a car pulled into the lot, decorated with Just Married in fading chalk paint on the windows. Jack and Meri emerged and were immediately surrounded by townspeople and the Barlow family. "Hey, Jack is back."

"Let's go say hi," Rachel said, because then she could put off the conversation she was having with Colton. The one where he asked her for more, and she had to decide if she wanted to take that risk.

She'd seen happy endings, and she'd seen heartbroken endings. What guarantee did she have that her own would be happy, like Jack and Meri? Or Luke and Peyton? Mac and Savannah?

"Rachel!" Meri broke out of the crowd and came over to Rachel, drawing her into a hug. "Just the person I wanted to see!"

Rachel had known Meri in high school, and had helped Meri over the years with finding gowns for her pageants. That had led Rachel into becoming a wedding planner, because she found she really enjoyed the planning, the shopping, the process of helping someone else create a fantasy. Now Meri was working as a photographer and settling into life in Stone Gap as Jack's wife. "Congratulations again. I hope you had a wonderful honeymoon."

"I definitely did." She smiled, the kind of secret smile that only women in the in-love club had. "If you want to marry a good man, marry a Barlow."

Rachel definitely wasn't thinking about marrying

anyone. Especially not Colton Barlow. Yet her gaze strayed to him, talking to Jack, the two brothers looking so much alike they could be twins. Luke and Mac joined them, the four brothers joking and laughing as if they'd been together all their lives. Colton had fit right in with his family, with this town. With her.

"So, are you still doing the wedding planning?" Meri asked.

"I…" Rachel saw her father, bustling in and out of the store, his arms filled with boxes of supplies. He looked energetic and excited and raring to get back to work. "Yeah. I am."

"That's awesome!" Meri grabbed Rachel's hands. "What do you think about joining forces? I'm trying to get my photography business off the ground, and I'd be glad to give your clients a break on my rate."

That would be a wonderful thing to offer in her wedding packages, and she knew Meri would do a terrific job. "That's awesome, Meri. Yes, definitely. And just in time, because Ginny wants me to plan her wedding."

"Great! I'm surprised I didn't hear about her engagement all the way in the Bahamas, given Ginny's power of publicity," Meri said. "I'd love to help you. It should be a win for both of us."

"I agree." The free advertising with Ginny spreading the word was yet another reason why handling the former debutante's wedding would be great for business. In that moment Rachel decided to take the leap. To call up Ginny, agree to take on the rushed, too-pink, too-loud wedding from hell and recharge her business in a big way. "It'll be awesome to work with you, Meri."

Meri drew Rachel into a one-armed hug and the two of them faced the quartet of Barlow men. "So, when are you going to be planning your own wedding? Don't give me that look. News of you and Colton did, in fact, reach the Bahamas." Meri laughed. "Blame Luke. For a former playboy, that man is a huge romantic."

"Let me just get back to the business of planning other people's happy endings," Rachel said. "And leave my own for…later."

"Uh-huh. If I remember right, I was saying the same thing myself a few months ago." Meri wagged her left hand and the sparkling diamond band sitting there now. "Things can change in a blink of an eye, so be ready."

Rachel let out a little laugh. "I've never felt less ready for change in my life."

Meri looked her in the eye. "If you ask me, that's the best time to fall in love."

Chapter Fourteen

Colton's mother Vanessa took the news poorly. She started to cry on the phone, saying she would never see her son again. Colton assured her he would visit Atlanta often and that Katie would drive down to see him and bring their mother along. His mother never had handled change well, but Colton hoped that without him to rely upon, she might finally be more inspired to take charge of her own life.

Katie, on the other hand, was overjoyed. "So, what's this town like? Lot of single men?"

Colton laughed. "I'm not exactly checking out those particular stats. But…there is one woman I really like."

"Oh, really?" Katie let out a low whistle. "I never thought I'd see the day when you considered settling down. I thought you said you didn't want to have any-one depending on you ever again."

"Rachel isn't like that. If anything, she's trying her best not to depend on me for anything at all. She's de-termined and stubborn and—"

"In love with you? Because you sure sound in love with her."

"Me? No. No way. We haven't known each other that long."

Katie laughed. "That is an awful lot of denials, big brother. I think you fell hard and fast, and I think she's part of the reason you're staying in that town."

"Maybe…" He wasn't going to give any more of an affirmative than that. For one, it was too soon, like he'd said.

On the other hand, he couldn't put Rachel from his mind. When he was standing right next to her, all he wanted to do was kiss her. When she was away from him, she lingered on the fringes of his every thought. He wondered what she was doing right now. On a Sat-urday in a town so small, someone could sneeze and they'd hear it on the other side of the street. Was she thinking of him? Was she out with friends? Walking the beach? Curled up in bed with a good book?

"Maybe?" Katie said. "Sounds pretty definite to me. I'm happy for you, though. Really happy."

"And a wee bit envious?"

"Maybe." His sister sounded a little distant. She usually kept whatever she was going through to her-self, and that made him worry about her.

"Why don't you come down and visit once I get

settled in for real?" Colton suggested. "And check out the single male population for yourself?"

Katie let out a faux gasp. "Are you telling this work-aholic to take a vacation?"

"I am indeed. An entire week would be great. Maybe even give you a minute to catch your breath."

Katie thought for a second. "Okay, I will, but only if you introduce me to this woman who has your head all ajumble."

"'Ajumble'? Is that even a word?"

"It is now." Katie laughed again. "All right, speaking of work, I have to get back to my job. I'll see you soon, big brother. Good luck with the new job."

Colton said goodbye then hung up. The sun had gone down, so work on the hardware store had come to a halt an hour ago. There were a few things to finish up first thing tomorrow, then the rest would wait for the shipment of replacement inventory. All in all, though, Ernie should be able to open up on Monday morning and get right back to work.

Colton should have been pleased with the work he had done, the changes he had brought to this little corner of the world, but something was missing. No, not something. Someone.

Was he really going to wait for her to come to him? Or was he just going to go take the risk, tell Rachel how he felt and then see where it went from there?

A few minutes later he was standing outside Rachel's apartment door. He knocked then waited, as nervous as a seventh grader heading to his first dance. She pulled open the door, looking sexier than he'd ever seen her in a pair of yoga pants and an oversize tee that hid her curves, but left his memory to fill in the blanks. "Sorry for coming by so late, but I really wanted to see you."

"It's fine." She smiled that dazzling smile that nearly took his breath away. "Do you want to come in?"

"I do. Very much." He pulled his hand out from behind his back. "These are for you. They're not as nice as the ones I got from the flower shop, but I picked these myself. I'm hoping they weren't anyone's in particular, or you are going to have a very angry Stone Gap resident on your door in the morning."

"They're beautiful." She took the bouquet of wildflowers, a jumble of pinks and purples and yellows, and brought it to her nose. "Where did you find them?"

"Remember that old, abandoned haunted house you showed me? I had seen them in the back of the house that night, and I thought that if flowers could grow in a place like that, one that had been neglected for so long, that maybe there was hope for anything to grow in this place. Or anyone. Like me." He stepped inside her apartment and nudged the door shut. He decided to just get straight to why he was there. No more delaying—hadn't he put everything on hold long enough? "I've gone a long time with just…standing still. I want more, Rachel."

"More? Like what more?"

"Like a future with you. I know it's too soon, and too fast, and a thousand other things, but I started falling for you hard from the very first day. I mean, how many women does a man meet who are beautiful, talented at fishing and fabulous shortstops?" He grinned. "You're one of a kind, Rachel Morris."

He'd realized on the way over here that he didn't want to lose her. He didn't, in fact, want to spend another day without her. He loved the way she lit his heart when she smiled, the way she asked more out of him and made him expect more of himself, the way she surprised him with things like the tour of the town or a little-known fact about herself. She was everything he'd always been looking for—even if he didn't realize that until he found it.

"A future?" Her eyes were wide, and she was shaking her head. "You're right. This is too soon and too fast and—"

"And what are you afraid of?"

She let out a gust. "There you go again, assuming everything is about me being afraid."

"Fight or flight, isn't that the old adage? Most of us either fight against what we don't want or run from it, but in almost all cases, that comes out of fear." He took her hands in his. "I'm scared as hell that I am going to screw this up with you. That you're going to look at me and think, *What am I doing with this clown?*"

She laughed. "I could never think that. For one, you don't have a red nose."

That made him laugh, too. It eased the tension in the room and all this seriousness of his. "I'm pretty sure I can buy one, if that's your thing."

"I have more of a thing for firefighters." A teasing grin lit her face, her eyes. "Especially ones who know how to fish."

"Whoops. Guess that rules me out." He held tight to her hands and inhaled the sweet scent of her perfume. "Unless you're okay with a slightly damaged firefighter who is eager to learn how to fish?"

She smiled up at him, one of those hundreds of smiles that he could draw in his sleep. "That could work."

"Good." He swept her into his arms and kissed her. A long, sweet kiss that seemed to make time stop. She tasted of vanilla and chocolate, like a candy that he had been long denied. And when she curved against his body, it was as if the missing piece he'd been looking for was fitting right there against his heart. Damn, he was falling, and falling hard for Rachel.

"So, what do you say we start the future simply?" he said. "Come with me to Bobby and Della's anniversary party tomorrow night. It's a casual thing, just close family and friends at the Sea Shanty."

She pulled out of his arms and crossed the room. "Colton, I don't know if we should have a future. I mean, you're right, this is moving fast and I am afraid. Who wouldn't be? We barely know each other. What if it doesn't work out? Do you know how many weddings I've gone to, only to see the divorce announcement in the paper before the year is up?"

"But how many have you gone to and that didn't happen?" he asked. "Rachel, there are no guarantees in life. There's only taking a chance."

"I don't like taking chances. I like to know what is coming tomorrow, and the next day, and the day after that." She let out a breath. "It's why…it's why I stayed at the store instead of keeping my business going. Part of that was for my dad, yes, but part of it was because I was scared that I could fail."

"Me, too, Rachel. I'm just as scared as you. But I'm tired of letting that fear rule all my decisions. Life is short," he said softly. "I don't want to live another minute of it being afraid."

"I know that, and tell myself I feel the same way, but when it comes to actually moving past those fears…" She bit her lip. "Working for yourself means taking a risk every single day. For me, that was like jumping out of a building every day. It scared me, and when I had a chance to stop doing that…I took it. Now I'm looking at being able to go back to my business, and frankly I'm scared as hell."

"Scared of succeeding? Or scared of failure?"

She let out a breath. "Both. And now you want me to take a chance with my heart. That's…even more fragile. And even scarier."

"You can't know, Rachel, if this will work out between us or not, if you don't take that chance." He took her hands again and drew her closer. "So take that chance with me."

Rachel had made up an excuse to avoid answering Colton's question, and to get him out of her apartment. Okay, yeah, it was the coward's way out, but she just needed some room to breathe, to think. She could see everything she'd ever wanted—ever dreamed of—within reach, yet she hesitated on going after it? What the heck was wrong with her?

"You're an idiot," Melissa said later that night, while she wrangled her squirmy baby back into a seated position and tried to give her son a bottle. He batted it away. "And I mean that in the nicest way."

"Gee, thanks." Rachel picked up one of the tiny T-shirts in the basket of clean laundry beside the armchair and folded it. Melissa's house was a comfortable mess, the kind of place that said *home*, with toys on the floor and a box of Cheerios on the counter, and the kids playing a video game on the TV across the room. "What made you say yes when Jason proposed?"

"Between you and me? A really good bottle of Chardonnay. I was just a tad—" she lowered her voice "—*tipsy* when he proposed. The next morning I woke up with a hangover and a total panic attack."

"You did? You never told me that." Rachel kept on folding. There was something cathartic about watching the jumbled laundry become straight, even piles.

"I did, indeed. I was a mess for about twenty-four hours," Melissa said. "I was so sure Jason and I would end up—" she lowered her voice again "—d-i-v-o-r-c-e-d, like my parents. And there was no way I wanted to go through that."

"Then what made you change your mind?"

"A Post-it note." Melissa let out a little laugh. "Jason had left me a note on my car the next morning, on a Post-it note, and he said sometimes the best things came out of what seemed like the biggest mistakes. And he told me to look up the story of those little sticky notes."

"Really?"

Melissa held up a hand. "Cross my heart. So I did

it. And do you know that the guy who invented them was actually trying to mix up a batch of glue, when he failed, or so he thought, and made an adhesive that could be applied and reapplied. It took him a bit, but then he thought of putting that glue on a piece of paper, and voilà, the sticky note was born. He took a risk, and it worked out pretty darn well for him."

"You got married because of that?"

"Well, that and the fact that Jason has a hot body and can—" she glanced at her kids "—uh, make me... happy like it's an Olympic sport." Melissa winked.

Rachel laughed. "I'm pretty sure it's that last one that swayed you the most."

"Honestly? It was the note. I had turned him down when he first proposed, but that man kept coming back. He refused to give up. He told me that we were meant to be, and he was going to spend the rest of his life proving it."

And he had, given how happy Melissa seemed. Yes, they had their stresses with the kids and the mortgage and life in general, but Rachel couldn't remember a day when she hadn't seen Melissa smiling. Every time her friend spoke about her husband, it was with that special little smile, the one that said she'd entered an exclusive club.

"That firefighter is a genuinely nice guy," Melissa said. "And he's worth a hundred sticky notes, if you ask me."

"But is it the right time?" Rachel started folding faster, as if increasing the pile of T-shirts and leggings would make the rest of her worried mind fall into order, too. "I'm debating whether to relaunch my business. I have Ginny's wedding, if I want to take that on, but what if that takes too much of my time or it fails or—"

Melissa put a hand on top of Rachel's, halting the furious folding. "There's always going to be a but and a what-if," she said. "And as much as I love the fact that you are taking care of my laundry tonight, I think you need to quit worrying and start doing. Because I think your biggest problem—and I mean this in the nicest way…"

"What?" Rachel prompted.

"You don't believe in the very thing you are creating." Melissa gave Rachel a wry smile. "You have to believe in happily-ever-after to pull it off successfully. Both for others and for yourself."

"I do believe in…" Rachel paused. "Okay, maybe I don't. I mean, look at my parents. Married for almost thirty years, and I don't know if they were ever truly happy. The Barlows—everyone would call Bobby and Della the happiest couple in this town, yet they went through a period where Bobby had someone else."

"But he came back to Della and has made a wonderful family here. He made a mistake. That's all."

"How many happy couples do we know, Melissa? Even in my business, at least a third of them end up divorced."

"That's not your fault."

"No, but it doesn't exactly make me believe that a ring is any kind of guarantee."

"It isn't." Melissa shrugged. "That's the truth of it. No ring or piece of paper or vow in front of a priest is any guarantee that your life together will be happy or that your marriage will last. All you can do is take that leap, have faith and then work like hell—" she glanced at her kids "—I mean, heck, at keeping it together."

Faith. It was what Rachel had told Colton to have. What she had seen in Winona and Charles's story. And the one thing it seemed she lacked. So she went on folding shirts and leggings and pretending that she wasn't mostly afraid that she was going to miss out on something wonderful if she didn't take that leap.

Chapter Fifteen

Dinner with the Barlow family was, apparently, always an adventure. That was one thing Colton learned pretty quickly. The Sunday meal was held a little earlier than usual, due to the anniversary party scheduled for that evening, but that didn't matter. And with Jack, Luke, Mac *and* Colton all in the same house, the entire event was raucous and loud and really gave Colton a feel for what it must have been like to have grown up in a house with dozens of siblings.

He loved every minute of it. He had seconds of the lasagna, he ate dessert and he joked with his brothers as if they had always been together.

Jack and Colton offered to wash the dishes while Mac and Luke cleaned up the dining room, leaving Bobby and Della to get ready for their party. Meri had left early, along with Luke and Mac's fiancées, to finish decorating the Sea Shanty for the event.

Jack started the water running then glanced over his shoulder to see if his parents had left the room. "Did you think Dad and my mom seemed a little off tonight?"

Bobby had been distracted at dinner, and Della had barely talked to her husband. They'd each talked to the boys, but the easy camaraderie that he'd witnessed before with Bobby and Della wasn't there. "Yeah. But then again, I don't know them well enough to know what normal is."

"Luke and Mac said Dad's been kind of distant lately, and that they've hardly seen Mom." Jack shook his head. "What happened in the week I was gone?"

"Nothing that I know of," Colton said. "Except for... well, except for me showing up in town. I'm sure it's been tough on your mother to have me around, a constant reminder of what happened years ago."

"Yeah, that could be it, but I'm not so sure. I just hope..." Jack let out a breath, and started loading the dishes into the soapy water. "I hope they work it out. They've got more than three decades together."

"You talking about Dad and Mom?" Luke said, as he set a pile of dirty plates on the counter. "Whatever's up, neither one of them is talking about it. But I heard..."

"What?" Jack said when Luke didn't finish.

"I don't know if I should even say anything." Luke let out a long breath.

"If you don't, I'll have to use the sprayer on you." Jack brandished the black nozzle.

Luke feigned fear and put his hands up to protect his hair. "Oh, no, not that. Anything but the sprayer!"

Jack laughed and slid it back into place. "Okay, okay, your hairdo is safe with me, Elvis. What did you hear?"

The tease dropped from Luke's face and his blue eyes filled with worry. "Mom has been talking to George Wilcox, the Realtor. She even went to see a few properties this week."

If Colton could have packed up and left town right that second, he would have. This was all his fault—he never should have come to town and upset the apple cart. Now he'd taken a job in Stone Gap, which meant he'd be a constant reminder to Della of what Bobby had done three decades ago. If their marriage broke up because of his presence—

"Maybe I should skip the party tonight," he said to his brothers.

"No, don't do that," Jack said. "I'm sure whatever this is with my parents will blow over before then. They've had fights before, but they always resolve them."

"I hope you're right," Colton said. He picked up a dish and dried it, then replaced it in the cabinet. He'd come to Stone Gap to make a change in his own life, but it seemed everywhere he turned, he was causing changes in other people's lives. And not necessarily the kind they wanted.

Bobby stood in the Sea Shanty and looked at his friends and his kids and wondered if he shouldn't just send them all home. He was supposed to be celebrating his thirty-fifth wedding anniversary, but it felt more like a funeral of his marriage. Della had barely talked to him all weekend, and when they'd first arrived, she'd gone off to talk to the local Realtor.

Bobby wasn't a smart man, but he was no moron, either. He knew what it meant if Della was looking at real estate. Now he just needed to confront her on it, before this party got too far underway. The last thing he wanted to do was stand around for four hours, letting people congratulate him on a marriage that was over.

He found Della standing on the outdoor deck, looking out at the water. She looked stunning tonight, in a sequined navy blue dress that skimmed her knees. She'd put her hair up and little curls dusted along her neck. She had on a pair of dangly earrings that swayed a bit in the breeze. "You look beautiful, Della," he said when he came up beside her.

She turned and smiled at him. "Why, thank you, Robert. You look dashing yourself. Exactly the same as the day we got married."

"Well, maybe a little more of me than the day we got married." He patted his belly beneath the button-down shirt and tie that felt more like a boa constrictor on his neck. But ties made Della happy, so he'd worn one without complaint.

"That's fine," she said. "There's more of you to love."

"Is there?" He screwed up his courage and let out a breath. "I saw you talking to George. I know you're hiding something from me and if you're leaving me,

Della, then just tell me straight out so we don't go through this sham—"

"I bought a house."

Bobby's heart shattered. He could have driven a samurai sword through his chest and it would have hurt less. "A…a house? When?"

"Yesterday. Don't worry, I didn't use our retirement savings. I used that money my mother left me when she died. I've had it in that CD for years, and it was just enough to buy the Richardson house."

The Richardson house? That dilapidated piece of crap about ready to cave in? "Wait. The one that Gareth guy owned? The one that's supposed to be haunted?"

"The very one." She gave him a grin, as pleased as the Cheshire cat.

"Why would you buy that place?"

"Because nothing does better marketing for a bed-and-breakfast in the South than a haunted house once owned by a suspected murderer. I know the place is a mess, but with Savannah's keen eye for restoration and Jack's amazing building skills we should be able—"

"Wait. Did you say bed-and-breakfast?" Bobby wondered if maybe he should get his hearing checked, because every word that came out of Della's mouth made little sense to him. "Why would you care about a B&B?"

"Because that's what I'm going to do," she said, and her Cheshire cat grin widened. "I'm going to renovate that house and run it as a B&B. I love cooking, I love keeping a house and I absolutely love company."

"And…" He took in a deep breath then pushed it out with the next words. "What about us?"

"What about us?" She looked at him, and then her eyes softened and her smile widened. "Oh, Robert Barlow, you big fool. You don't think you can get rid of me that easily, do you? I've been with you thirty-five years. I've barely got you broken in. I'm not going anywhere. Nowhere at all."

He laughed, a big whoop of a laugh that scared a nearby seagull and seemed to echo across the ocean. Then he took the love of his life into his arms and gave her a long, hot, deep kiss.

"My, my, Robert," Della said, a sweet red flush in her cheeks, "you still do surprise me."

"And you, my dear wife, still surprise me." He brushed a tendril of hair off her forehead then cupped her cheek. "Thank you for the best thirty-five years of my life. I can't wait for the next thirty-five."

She leaned her head against his shoulder and fit into the place where she had always been happiest, right in Bobby's arms. "I can't, either. But I can promise you one thing. They're going to be an adventure."

"They will indeed," Bobby whispered, then kissed his wife again, softly, sweetly and with a whole lot of gratitude in his heart.

The Sea Shanty was filled to the brim by the time Rachel arrived at the party. She was late, but only because she had changed her dress three times, then at the last minute invited her father along for moral support.

"You look beautiful," her father said. He gave his daughter's arm a pat. "Your mother would be so proud."

"Oh, thank you, Dad." Rachel pressed a kiss to her

father's cheek then headed into the dining room. She saw Della and Bobby sitting at the head table set up by the window, flanked by their sons and their wives and fiancées. An empty seat sat to the left of Colton.

When she entered the room, he looked up and smiled at her. Even from here, all the way across the restaurant, a simple smile from him sent a flutter through her heart. She wanted to close that distance and leap into his arms and forget every silly fear she'd ever had.

There was a band on the stage and they launched into a version of "At Last." Bobby got to his feet and put out his hand to his wife. Della blushed then took his hand and went with him to the dance floor.

Rachel watched them, two people still happy together after three and a half decades of marriage, still laughing, still blushing when they flirted. They spun around the dance floor, a testament to taking that leap and making it work.

"Shall we dance?"

Colton's warm voice in her ear slid through her like butter. She could feel a blush filling her own face, and for a brief moment wondered if thirty-five years from now, that would be them in the middle of the dance floor.

"I thought you'd never ask," she said, then slipped into his arms. She fit perfectly against him, and they moved as if they'd been made for dancing together. As they waltzed past Bobby and Della, Della gave Rachel and Colton a smile.

"You two make a wonderful couple," Della said.

"I keep trying to tell her that," Colton said to Della, then he turned back to Rachel. "When are you going to believe me?"

She drew in a deep breath. Either she took this risk or she risked something even bigger—losing this incredible man. "How about tonight?" she said.

"Really?" A wide grin filled his face. "What changed your mind?"

"It was a desk." Rachel swayed with Colton to the right, their movements easy and fluid with the music. She could see the confusion in his face, and that made her happy that he didn't realize how one simple thing had changed everything. "On the way over here, I stopped by the store with my dad to see what you guys had done this morning. He wanted to see if the shop would be ready to open on Monday and it is. We need to wait on some inventory, of course, but there's enough to get started back up again. So thank you for all your hard work and turning that around so fast."

"That was my intention," Colton said. "I know business has been slow and I didn't want him to lose too much business because of being closed down for too long."

Yet another vote in the thoughtful and considerate column for Colton Barlow, she thought.

"Then I go into the break room," Rachel went on, "and I see the ice-maker line and the new refrigerator, and the new doorway all complete, and then I see—" even now, thinking about it made her smile, heck, even choked her up a little "—a desk in the corner. A small one, with a little set of bookshelves above it. And a small sign over the top, carved out of a piece of wood. With my name on it, and the words Wedding Planner after it. You wouldn't know of a certain firefighter responsible for that desk and that sign, would you?"

He shrugged, and she swore she saw a blush in his cheeks. "I know it's going to be hard for you to leave your dad. And that you probably want to take things slow with your business and easing him back into work. So I set up a little space for you in the back of the shop, so you can run your business and be close to him if he needs you."

She had told herself she wouldn't cry today, but tears welled in her eyes all the same. Colton had truly thought of everything, and she knew she could never thank him enough. "How do you know me so well, so quickly, Colton Barlow?"

"I think because we're two of a kind." He stopped dancing with her and reached up to cup her jaw and meet her gaze. "We both are so committed to taking care of the people around us that we forget about ourselves. I wanted you to be able to have everything you wanted, Rachel, whether or not you were with me."

That was the moment when Rachel fell in love with Colton. When she'd seen that desk and realized that he only wanted what was best for her, what would make her happy. Even if he wasn't part of that picture. "You are an incredible man," she said.

"Only because I'm in love with an incredible woman." He traced her lips with his thumb, and she ached to kiss him, to never stop kissing him. "I know it's crazy, Rachel, but I am in love with you. I have loved you since that first day of the twenty-five-cent tour when you showed me that old house and you were so sentimental and sweet and—"

She rose on her toes and kissed him. To heck with the crowd dancing around the two fools standing still in the middle of the floor. "I love you, too," she said. Because she couldn't wait another second to say the words.

The smile on his face beamed as bright as the sun. "You know this is crazy, right?"

"It is, indeed. It's like the kind of fairy tales I create for my brides. But sometimes," she said softly, "sometimes, those fairy tales end in happily-ever-after."

Colton looked over at Della and Bobby, dancing to celebrate more than three decades of marriage. They were joined by Jack and Meri, then Luke and Peyton and finally Mac and Savannah. The dance floor was filled with people in love, people who had taken that risk and found something worth having on the other side.

"They do, indeed," he said, then he took Rachel into his arms and together, they joined the dance.

* * * * *

COMING NEXT MONTH FROM

H HARLEQUIN®

SPECIAL EDITION

Available June 21, 2016

#2485 MARRIAGE, MAVERICK STYLE!

Montana Mavericks: The Baby Bonanza • by Christine Rimmer

Tessa Strickland is *done* with hotshot men like billionaire Carson Drake. But after they wake up together following the Rust Creek Falls Baby Parade, Carson isn't willing to let the brunette beauty go without a fight. Especially when they might have their own baby bonanza from that night they don't quite remember...

#2486 THE BFF BRIDE

Return to the Double C • by Allison Leigh

Brilliant scientist Justin Clay and diner manager Tabby Taggart were best friends for decades, until one night of passion ruined everything. Now Justin is back in Weaver for work, and Tabby can't seem to stop running into him at every turn. With their "just friends" front crumbling, Justin must realize all the success he's dreamed of doesn't mean much without the girl he's always loved.

#2487 THIRD TIME'S THE BRIDE!

Three Coins in the Fountain • by Merline Lovelace

Dawn McGill has left two fiancés at the altar already, terrified her marriage will turn as bitter as her parents'. CEO Brian Ellis is wary of Dawn's past when he hires her as a nanny, not wanting his son to suffer another loss after the death of his mother. But Brian can't help the growing attraction he feels to the vibrant redhead. Is the third time really the charm for these two lonely hearts?

#2488 PUPPY LOVE FOR THE VETERINARIAN

Peach Leaf, Texas • by Amy Woods

A freak snowstorm leaves June Leavy and the puppies she rescued stranded at the Peach Leaf veterinary office, forcing her to spend the night there with Ethan Singh. Bad breakups have burned them both, leaving them with scars and shattered dreams. They're determined to find homes for the puppies, but can they find a home with each other along the way?

#2489 THE MATCHMAKING TWINS

Sugar Falls, Idaho • by Christy Jeffries

The Gregson twins long for a new mommy. So when they overhear their father, former navy SEAL captain Luke Gregson, admit to an attraction to their favorite local cop, Carmen Delgado, they come up with a plan to throw the two adults together. But will the grown-ups see beyond their painful pasts to a new chance at love and a family?

#2490 HIS SURPRISE SON

The Men of Thunder Ridge • by Wendy Warren

Golden boy Nate Thayer returns home to discover that time hasn't dimmed his desire for Izzy Lambert, the girl he once loved and lost. But can Izzy, a girl from the wrong side of the tracks, trust that this time Nate is here to stay...especially when he discovers the secret she's been keeping for years?

YOU CAN FIND MORE INFORMATION ON UPCOMING HARLEQUIN® TITLES,
FREE EXCERPTS AND MORE AT WWW.HARLEQUIN.COM.

HSECNM0616

He resisted the urge to tip up her chin and make her meet his eyes again. "So you're not mad at me for moving in here?"

And then she did look at him. God. He wished she would never look away. "No, Carson. I'm not mad. How long are you staying?"

"Till the nineteenth. I have meetings in LA the week of the twentieth."

She touched him then, just a quick brush of her hand on the bare skin of his forearm. Heat curled inside him, and he could have sworn that actual sparks flashed from the point of contact. Then she confessed, her voice barely a whisper, "I regretted saying goodbye to you almost from the moment I hung up the phone yesterday."

"Good." The word sounded rough to his own ears. "Because I'm going nowhere for the next two weeks."

She slanted him a sideways glance. "You mean that I'm getting a second chance with you whether I want one or not?"

All possible answers seemed dangerous. He settled on "Yes."

"I… Um. I want to take it slow, Carson. I want to…" She glanced down—and then up to meet his eyes full-on again. "Don't laugh."

He banished the smile that was trying to pull at his mouth. "I'm not laughing."

"I want to be friends with you. Friends first. And then we'll see."

Friends. Not really what he was going for. He wanted so much more. He wanted it all—everything that had happened Monday night that he couldn't remember. He wanted her naked, pressed tight against him. Wanted to coil that wild, dark hair around his hand, kiss her breathless, bury himself to the hilt in that tight, pretty body of hers, make her beg him to go deeper, hear her cry out his name.

But none of that was happening right now. So he said the only thing he could say, given the circumstances. "However you want it, Tessa."

"You're sure about that?"

"I am."

"Because I'm…" She ran out of steam. Or maybe courage.

And that time he did reach out to curl a finger beneath her chin. She resisted at first, but then she gave in and lifted her gaze to his once more. He asked, "You're what?"

"I'm not good at this, you know?" She stared at him, her mouth soft and pliant, all earnestness, so sweetly sincere. "I'm kind of a doofus when it comes to romance and all that."

Turn your love of reading into rewards you'll love with

Harlequin My Rewards

**Join for FREE today at
www.HarlequinMyRewards.com**

Earn **FREE BOOKS** of your choice.

Experience **EXCLUSIVE OFFERS** and contests.

Enjoy **BOOK RECOMMENDATIONS**
selected just for you.

PLUS! Sign up now
and get **500** points
right away!

Earn
FREE
REWARDS
Join
Today!
HarlequinMyRewards.com

MYR16R

THE WORLD IS BETTER WITH

Romance

Harlequin has everything from contemporary, passionate and heartwarming to suspenseful and inspirational stories.

Whatever your mood,
we have a romance just for you!

Connect with us to find your next great read,
special offers and more.

Love the Harlequin book you just read?

Your opinion matters.

Review this book on your favorite book site, review site, blog or your own social media properties and share your opinion with other readers!

Be sure to connect with us at:
Harlequin.com/Newsletters
Facebook.com/HarlequinBooks
Twitter.com/HarlequinBooks